MURDEROUS CRAFT

SAM CHEEVER

ELECTRIC PROSE PUBLICATIONS

Dead End Job: When the only thing on tap is death.

A corpse in the bathroom of a popular bar. An old acquaintance still nursing a mad-on from fifteen years earlier. And a cast of characters possessing secrets they'll do almost anything to keep. It's enough to make reformed (sort of) party girl Blaise Runa want to quit her dead end job. But in the meantime she fully intends to grab her sexy private eye fiancée and dig into the mess. Because she might be trying to *adult*, but that doesn't mean she's gotten any less nosy!

1

*I*f looks could kill, the woman across the bar would have already butchered Blaise and hacked her into a million tiny pieces. Something about her seemed familiar, but Blaise couldn't put a name to the face to save her life.

She narrowed her gaze at the woman and picked up another freshly washed wine glass, running a towel over the clear glass to dry it.

"Who you glarin' at brown sugar?"

Blaise held the hostile gaze across the room. "That chick's been glowering at me. I'm just trying to figure out who she is."

Tyrese Miller leaned an arm on Blaise's shoulder and followed her line of sight to the spot near the door. "I don't see anybody glarin' at you, Blaise."

Blaise slid the wine glass into the rack above her head. "That's because she just left."

Her boss lifted a dense, black eyebrow. "Mm-hm."

She turned a grin on him. "I'm not lyin'."

He chuckled darkly. "It was probably just some woman whose husband lusts after you, brown sugar. I wouldn't pay her no mind."

Blaise shrugged. "She seemed familiar but I can't come up with a name."

"Bronislava?"

Blaise frowned. "Huh?"

"That's a name. Here's another one. Shampooya." His trademark grin widened, showing a full mouth of straight white teeth except for a single gold one on the bottom. "Am I ringing a bell?"

She snorted. "I think your bell's already been rung. Those aren't names, Ty. Those are letters you shoved together to create nonsense."

He held up a hand. "God's truth. I saw 'em in a baby names book. They're real names."

"What in the world were you doing looking through a baby names book?" She lifted her brows. "Is there somethin' you need to tell me?"

Grabbing a frosty glass mug, Ty pulled a draft beer and settled it on the counter for the waitress swaying in his direction. "My brother's expecting. Well...his wife is...and they're having trouble picking a name."

"Hopefully they're not desperate enough to ask for your help."

"They have and I'm coming through for them. They now have a long, long list of intriguing names to select from. Personally, I'm leaning toward Exaltacion."

"Good Lord."

"Hey, it's biblical."

"So was The Plague of Locusts. Equally catastrophic."

The waitress reached the bar and grinned when she saw the beer sitting there. "Thanks, Ty." She was petite, curvy and sported a thick nest of dark brown hair which she was currently wearing loose and wavy around her shoulders. The waitress winked at the bar's owner. "How'd you know I was coming for that?"

He ran a cloth over a wet spot on the bar. "I've told ya a million times, Suz, I know all and see all."

Suzie Whotsnoggin turned a bright blue gaze on Blaise, widening it comically. "The man's delusional."

Laughing, Ty moved down the bar to help a customer.

Blaise grinned at her best friend. "How you doin' Suz?"

The waitress shrugged. "Okay. Tips are good tonight. But I'm dead tired. We didn't get out of here until three this morning. I swear, something's changed. We've never been this busy."

"I know, right? It must be this new line of local

beers. I think people like the idea of supporting the small breweries."

"Hey, gorgeous, where's my beer?" a masculine voice called across the bar.

Suz rolled her eyes. "*Doodie* calls." She picked up the frosted mug of beer. "You want to go shopping tomorrow? It's my first day off in over a week and I want to do something fun."

"I'll see what Dolfe's doing. If he's working I'd love to go. Mama needs a new pair of shoes."

"Doesn't Mama always?" Suz asked before swinging away. She swayed across the bar with the beer, large gold hoops in her ears dancing with her movement. Blaise watched, amused, as she deftly sidestepped her rude customer's groping hands.

Shaking her head, Blaise fought the coil of discomfort in her gut. She'd loved the atmosphere, lights, music and fun of working at *Tyrese's Bar*. But after six months some of the bloom was starting to wear off. To her ever-growing surprise, Blaise was starting to think she'd like to do something else. Something that would leave her nights free to spend with her honey, Dolfe. At least when he wasn't scoping out some cheating spouse or elusive thug.

Dolfe Honeybun was a private investigator who worked closely with the Indianapolis Metropolitan Police Department on the occasional case. He was darn good at his job and Blaise loved that he was *that* kind of guy. A big, strong man who carried a gun and an attitude and didn't take any crap from anybody. But between his hours and hers, they didn't get to spend nearly enough time together.

And since they'd only been affianced a few months. That was a serious problem.

"You're Blaise Runa aren't you?"

Blaise's head snapped up and her pulse spiked. She hadn't even heard the woman approach. "Oh my gosh! You startled me."

The woman didn't seem to care. She slid a hostile gaze over Blaise and frowned. "You don't remember me do you?"

"I'm really trying to." It probably wasn't a good sign that the most memorable thing about the woman was her frown. "Did I...annoy...you in some way?"

"You could say that. If sleeping with my boyfriend can be classified as an annoyance."

Kerplunk! The memory fell into place. Blaise leaned closer, narrowing her eyes at her accuser. The years since High School hadn't been kind...but Blaise could almost see the pretty face she once knew beneath the bags and wrinkles. "Dierdre?"

The woman put her hands on her well-padded hips and glowered up at Blaise. "You admit you slept with him?"

Blaise couldn't believe it was the same woman she'd been so terrified of. Voted most likely to irritate a rich husband. Head cheerleader. Came from a wealthy family who gave her everything she wanted. She seemed much smaller than she had back then.

Well...shorter anyway.

"I never slept with Roger White."

"Of course you did!"

Blaise shook her head, cocking a hip against the bar and crossing her arms over her middle. "Nope. We were just friends."

Dierdre Masterson slapped her hands on the bar top and leaned closer, wafting rancid breath that smelled like garlic into Blaise's face. "You must have slept with Roger!"

Conversations all around them stopped. All eyes turned to Dierdre and, by proximity, Blaise. Fortunately Blaise didn't embarrass easily. She chuckled. "I'm sorry to disappoint, Dierdre. I didn't."

"Then why did he break up with me!" she wailed.

The curious gazes slid quickly away, clearly unwilling to witness the train wreck at the bar. Blaise figured they'd hoped for salacious details but weren't comfortable watching Dierdre debase herself.

"I don't know the answer to that," Blaise said softly. "You'll have to ask him."

"I was going to ask him," the other woman said despondently. "But he stood me up."

Blaise stared at the lumpy woman sitting across the bar. She frowned, and then felt anger finally rise. "You asked him here to confront me?"

Dierdre Masterson shrugged. "I figured I'd be able to tell from the expression in his face when he looked at you."

"Good God, D, that was eleven years ago. You need to get over it."

The other woman's eyes filled with tears and Blaise instantly regretted yelling at her. "Would you like a drink? We have some really great local beers..."

Dierdre grimaced. "Not beer. I have enough of that at work."

Blaise's eyebrows shot upward. "You don't say?"

Seeing her expression, Dierdre laughed. She swiped tears off her round cheeks, sniffling. "I work at *Byerson's Beers.*"

Understanding flared. "Ah. Those beers are some of our best sellers. Great stuff."

Dierdre didn't look like she cared. "Whatever." She sat in silence for a long moment and then glanced at Blaise. "What's wrong with me? Why can't I keep a man?"

Blaise panicked. The last thing she wanted to do was give counseling to a woman she didn't even really like. "Um..."

"Can I get you something to eat or drink?" Ty asked Dierdre. He winked at Blaise as he approached, nudging her to the side and putting himself between the pathetic woman on the other side of the bar and Blaise.

She could have kissed him.

"I don't want anything," Dierdre told him. Then she blinked and grabbed her purse. "Actually, you can do one thing for me. Have you seen this man today?"

She slid a photo across the bar to Ty. Blaise looked over his shoulder and was shocked to see a picture of Roger White in his quarterback's uniform.

"He's older now, of course. That was in High School."

Ty's lips twitched and Blaise surreptitiously pinched him below the bar. "Ow! Erm, no I don't think..." He picked the photo up, studying it more carefully. "Actually, I think I might have."

Blaise barely resisted blowing a disbelieving raspberry. He was clearly just humoring the woman.

Dierdre's scowl turned upside down and she looked almost pretty as she smiled. "Really? He was here?"

"Still should be," Ty said, jerking his head toward the restrooms. "I saw him head to the *Men's* a while ago."

"How long?" Blaise asked. "I've been here an hour and I haven't seen him."

Ty glanced at his watch and frowned. "You're right. It's been a while. I hope he's okay in there."

"Did he seem ill?"

Ty thought about it. "He seemed fine when I saw

him. He was even chatting up a pretty young woman a while ago."

Grimacing, Dierdre climbed down from her stool. "I'd better go check on him."

"You can't...um...ma'am..." When Dierdre ignored him, Ty widened his eyes at Blaise.

"I'll stop her." She rounded the bar just as the door across the room opened and a short, balding man with a veiny nose staggered out, looking like he'd seen a ghost. He lifted round, brown eyes to Ty and flapped a hand. "There's...oh God...I think that guy in there is dead."

2

*B*laise stood near the door and tried to peer under the stall partition. "Who is it?" she asked the tall, sharp-eyed detective examining the scene. Brita Muldane pulled a wallet out of the man's pocket using a latex glove to keep from adding her own prints. Snapping it open, she perused the man's license. "Name's Roger M. White." She glanced up. "Is that the guy?"

A teeth-rattling shriek went up behind Blaise and she jumped.

Brita lifted slender, light brown brows. "I'll take that as a yes." She shoved the wallet into an evidence bag and tugged something from his shirt pocket.

"What's that?" Blaise asked.

"Electronic cigarette. Mr. White was apparently trying to quit."

Blaise's attention was locked on the dark-haired

corpse sprawled at the base of the toilet. His sight-less gaze was focused on the door, and one hand reached in her direction, fingers slightly curved, as if he'd died asking someone for help. She remembered he used to smoke cigarettes, and other stuff, in high school. "Can you tell what killed him?"

Brita crouched down and pulled his leather jacket away from his midsection. "No obvious wounds." She pointed to a crusty substance on his face. "Looks like he threw up. That broken blood vessel in his eye tells me it was violent." She straightened, flinging the glove into the trash as a commotion started behind Blaise. "That's probably CSU."

Blaise turned to find two men rolling a gurney through the bar. "EMTs." A tall man with longish, curly blond hair, a square chin and piercing green eyes came through the front door and held it open for a guy wearing the familiar polo and khakis of the CSU guys. "And the crime scene techs."

Brita nodded, moving toward the door. "Dolfe called me on the way over. He said he'd be here as soon as he could get away. He had a client in his office."

"I'm here now," the tall, handsome guy told Brita in his deep, sexy voice.

Blaise smiled up at him. "Hey handsome, want a date?"

Dolfe waggled blond brows. "Absolutely. But first

I have to help my girl. She's gotten herself embroiled in another suspicious death."

Blaise pouted playfully. "I'm sure it's not your girl's fault. She was just in the wrong place at the wrong time."

He shook his head, glancing at Brita. "What do you think, Brita? Is it murder?"

The attractive detective pushed past Blaise, forcing her to step out of the doorway. "Too early to tell." She nodded toward the EMTs. "You can go ahead and take the body. I've got what I need from him."

Brita waited until they'd rolled the gurney into the bathroom before indicating with a jerk of her head for Dolfe and Blaise to follow her across the bar.

Ty looked up as they passed, his gaze widening in silent question. Blaise lifted a hand to let him know she'd talk to him in a minute. He reluctantly returned his attention to Dierdre, who was babbling tearfully about the great love she and Roger had shared.

Funny, that wasn't how Blaise remembered it.

Brita stopped in a quiet spot at the back, behind the pool tables. She glanced toward the front, where all ten of the patrons who'd been in the bar when the body was discovered waited with worried expressions. Two uniforms stood near the door to keep them all there.

"Until I get the ME's report I'm going with poisoning on this one."

Blaise threw Ty a worried glance. "I don't like hearing that."

Brita shook her head. "I'll know more once he's been autopsied. But the signs are clear. The only question is when he was dosed and what he was dosed with."

"And who dosed him," Dolfe added helpfully.

Brita narrowed her pretty golden-brown gaze at him. "Yeah, that too."

Dolfe frowned thoughtfully. "Any idea when he got here?" he asked Blaise.

"Not a clue. I didn't see him."

"You came in around five this afternoon?" he asked.

"Right. I walked through the door at four forty-five. About thirty minutes later I saw Dierdre..."

Brita held up a hand. "Dierdre? Who's that?"

Blaise pointed to the woman sitting at the table with Ty. She had her head on the table and was full on sobbing. Ty looked like he wanted to gouge his own eyes out. "She was supposed to meet Roger here."

"You know her?" Brita asked.

"Yeah. From high school. I knew both of them." It suddenly hit her that Roger...her friend...was dead. Tears burned her eyes and she hurriedly scrubbed them away. Dolfe dropped an arm around her shoulders and pulled her close. "Roger and I were friends," she told him. "He dated Dierdre for a while."

"Could this be a lover's spat?"

Blaise shook her head. "I doubt it. I don't think they've seen each other for years." She threw Dierdre a worried look and Dolfe noticed. "What's wrong?"

Blaise briefly considered lying but quickly discarded the notion. She knew she hadn't done anything wrong but not telling the full truth would make her look guilty anyway. "Somebody's probably going to tell you that she and I argued."

Dolfe's jaw tightened. "Why would they tell me that?"

She bit her lip. "Because we kind of did."

"Blaise..."

She frowned up at him. "I was just minding my own business and she got all up in my grill."

"What did you argue about?" Brita asked, typing into her pda.

Blaise hated when Brita typed notes during their conversations. It felt way too much like an interrogation. "You don't need to type that. It was just a slight misunderstanding."

"About what?" Brita asked, giving Blaise cop eyes.

Blaise sighed. "About Roger. We fought about the dead guy."

D olfe sat back and watched the interaction in the room. At Brita's request, he'd separated everyone as best he could in the limited space, but communication still ran rampant through the place. Telling looks passed between the patrons...a widening of a gaze here, a rolling of the eyes there. One guy had a smug grin on his face as if he had a secret nobody else did.

Dolfe intended to have a little chat with that man at the earliest opportunity. After all, his mama had taught him it wasn't nice to keep secrets.

The only person in the room who didn't seem connected was the lean young man standing near the wall at the end of the bar. He wore a faded blue-gray uniform and a ball cap with the words *OnPoint Distributors* on the front. The man leaned on his hand truck and stared at the floor, his posture filled with tension.

Dolfe threw another look toward Blaise and Brita. The two of them had their heads together at a table in the far corner, out of earshot of the rest of the bar, and Brita was busily typing up notes, nodding occasionally at something Blaise said.

He slid a worried gaze over his honey, noting the taut posture and shiny gaze that told him more than anything how upset she was by the murder. He hated to see her upset and hated even more that

Brita had put him to work so he couldn't be there for her.

Not that Blaise generally needed him to lean on. At five feet ten inches tall, with the softest brown skin, playful brown eyes made exotic with a sexy tilt, and a lush mouth that mostly sent trouble into the air when it was open, she was like an Amazonian goddess with mad social skills and an abundance of brains which she tended to use only sparingly.

She was an ex party girl who was working hard at being serious because they were about to get married and she wanted to be a good wife and partner.

Dolfe was aware of how hard it was to change her pretty stripes and tried to soften it by meeting her halfway whenever he could. But he worried that she'd resent him for the change and was concerned over how it might affect them every day.

"Excuse me, sir?"

Dolfe snapped out of his thoughts and turned to the delivery guy. "Hey. What's up?"

Close up, the man was even younger than Dolfe had thought. He had wideset, clear blue eyes and a largish nose that currently sported a bright red zit on the very tip. A messy fringe of dirty blond hair stuck out from under the ball cap. He glanced toward Brita and frowned. "How much longer do you think this is gonna take? I'm gonna get in trouble with my boss if I don't make my other deliveries tonight."

"I'm sure your boss will understand. This is a murder investigation."

The man shook his head. "He don't understand nothin' except that if I'm s'posed to get to a place at nine I get there at nine, or earlier if possible."

Dolfe shook his head. "It's like that, is it?"

The guy looked miserable.

"I'll tell ya what. You give me your boss's number and I'll have a little talk with him."

The delivery guy's eyes went wide. "Oh no. He'll kill me for sickin' you on him."

"You don't really have a choice. Like I said, this is a murder investigation. If you don't do as you're asked you'll end up downtown in an interrogation room. That would really wreak havoc on your schedule wouldn't it."

The kid's shoulders slumped. He dug in his pocket and came up with a battered business card with a couple of splotches on it that looked suspiciously like catsup and mustard. Dolfe nodded. "Thanks. I'll give him a call later. Until then, how about you fill me in on what you know about tonight?"

The kid paled until only the enormous pimple still had color in it. If anything it looked even more red, like all the blood from the kid's cheeks had fled there. "I don't know nothin'. I just delivered my beer and was on the way out when the cops showed up."

He frowned. "If I'd only moved a little faster I could of got out before they stopped me."

Dolfe barely kept from grinning over the sentiment. He didn't want to encourage the kid. "You didn't see the guy before he went into the bathroom?"

The kid shrugged. "I might have. It's not like I know any of these people."

Dolfe settled back in his chair, stretching his long legs and crossing them at the ankles. His message was clear. He had all the time in the world.

The kid's frown deepened. "Look, I was only here a few minutes. I dropped the cases of beer on the end of the bar like always..."

"How often do you deliver here...?" Dolfe shook his head. "Sorry. I didn't catch your name."

The kid clearly didn't want to give Dolfe his name but he finally wrenched it out from between gritted teeth. "Nathan Lord."

"Nathan. Do you drop your product here often?"

He shrugged. "A couple times a week. Lately more like three times."

Dolfe whistled. "That's a lot of beer deliveries." He looked around. "This isn't a very big bar."

Some of the kid's hostility fled and a proud smile softened it. "We distribute some of the biggest sellers in the city."

"Really?" Dolfe's eyes went wide. "Tell me about the beer. I'm always looking for a new favorite."

"Well, *Byerson Beers* has a really nice craft beers that are pretty popular downtown. But we don't sell a lot of the darker beers here at *Tyrese's*."

"What do you sell here?"

"For microbrews I deliver mostly *Artisan Beers*. They have a couple in particular that are popular with the Millennials. If you like dark and hoppy they have a craft beer called Hoppa Long that's real popular. In fact it's one of our best sellers. Then there's Habitude. It's lighter, with a fruity finish but it's definitely habit forming like the name says."

"You sound like you speak from experience."

Nathan grinned. "I've been known to down a few mugs of the stuff."

Dolfe nodded, fighting a grin. "I hate to admit it but I like a fruity finish."

"Hey man, nothin' to be ashamed about. I seen two grown men fighting over the last bottle once. The stuff's seriously addictive."

"I'll check it out."

The kid nodded, some of the wariness leaving him.

"Since you're here so often, maybe you've seen our dead guy around?" Dolfe held up his phone with the picture he'd snapped of Mr. White on the bathroom floor. "Recognize him?"

The kid grimaced and pulled away before leaning closer. "He's dead?"

"He certainly is."

"I ain't never seen a dead guy before."

"Does he look familiar?"

"Well, I'm sure he looked different when he was alive and stuff."

"And stuff, yeah."

"But no. I'd have remembered him. He's a big guy."

Dolfe wasn't sure what the guy's size had to do with anything. "That's too bad. We're trying to establish what happened to him while he was here."

"How'd he die?" Nathan asked.

"We're not sure."

Nathan nodded. "Well, good luck with that, man."

Dolfe handed the kid one of his business cards. "If you think of anything that might help."

Nathan took the card, jamming it into the pocket of his jeans. "Yeah, I'll call. But don't hold your breath. I don't even know that dead dude."

Dolfe watched the kid slink away and return to his hand truck, looking eminently uncomfortable in his own skin. He knew the type. They put their heads down and went through life hoping not to bump up against anybody else for fear the other person's troubles would rub off on them. It was entirely possible that Nathan Lord had walked right past the dead guy and hadn't even seen him.

But given the timing of the thing, Dolfe doubted it.

"You helpin' that pretty cop?"

Dolfe looked over into the grizzled face of the patron seated a couple of tables away. The man had been cautioned a couple of times for yelling across the bar to his buddies. His gaze was assessing as it slid over Dolfe. "Detective Muldane doesn't need my help. She's perfectly capable of figuring this out herself."

The man's smile was mean. "You hittin' that? Or are you partial to the tall brown one. She looks like she knows what to do with a man."

Dolfe's good humor slid away and he fought an urge to bunch his hands into fists. He stood up and moved toward the man, stopping just inside the other guy's personal space and glaring down at him. It was gratifying to see some of the guy's bravado bleed away when he realized how big Dolfe was up close and personal. "I don't think you want to disrespect those women," he growled softly. Dolfe leaned closer, putting one hand flat on the table top and one on the back of Grizzly Asshat's chair. "Do you understand me?"

The man blinked and then lifted his hands. They were stained yellow on the ends as if he were a heavy smoker. He also wore the stench of old tobacco in his clothes and breath as he tried to laugh off his disgusting comments. "Hey man, chillax. I didn't mean nothin' by that."

"Actually," Dolfe told him, "words do mean

things." He straightened up and gave the man a cold smile. "But since I'm here, why don't you and I have a little chat?"

"About what?" Strangely, the man did not look happy at the prospect.

Dolfe lowered himself into the chair next to Grizzly and fixed the other man with an unwavering stare. "Let's start with whether you knew the deceased." He showed the other man the photo on his phone.

Unlike the kid, the older man barely blinked at the picture. He coughed wetly behind a meaty fist and shook his head. "Never seen him before."

Dolfe nodded, settling the phone on the table in front of him. "You sure about that?"

The guy didn't glance down again as he nodded.

"This bar isn't that big. I'd think all you regulars would get to know one another pretty quickly."

The other man shrugged. "That guy's not a regular."

Lifting his brows, Dolfe leaned in. "How do you know?"

"Because I am and I'd have seen him around if he was." He pointed a beefy finger at the picture. "I've never set eyes on that guy before. Or his girlfriend."

"Girlfriend?"

Grizzly pointed at Blaise. "I overheard that other

woman accuse the pretty brown lady of stealing her man."

"You may call her Miss Runa."

The man lowered bushy black and gray brows. "Huh?"

"That's her name. It's how you show respect to others. You use their names."

The man shrugged.

"When you say, other woman, who do you mean?" Dolfe asked.

Grizzly pointed to Dierdre Masterson. "The one screachin' like a cat with its tail on fire. Apparently she was supposed to meet the dead guy here."

Narrowing his gaze on the man, Dolfe sat back in his chair. "You sure know a lot about other people's business..." He cocked his head. "I didn't catch your name."

"Alvin Sparks." He swung a beefy arm as if to encompass the entirety of the bar. "I been comin' to this bar for almost ten years. I know most everybody in it. Well..." His lips twisted as if he'd just tasted a lemon. "Most everybody. Since Tyrese started carryin' fancy beer there's been lots of folks comin' around I don't know."

Dolfe allowed himself to smile. "I take it you're not a fan of Hoppa Long dark ale?"

The man blew a messy raspberry. "Girly beer. I drink good old American brew." He lifted a mug containing not much more than a dried foam ring and glowered into it. "I sure could use a refill. Maybe the pretty bro..." He blinked as Dolfe's big hand fisted on the table. "Um...Miss Runa could get it for me."

"Miss Runa's busy right now."

A small hand dropped onto Dolfe's shoulder. He looked up into Suzie Whotsnoggin's pretty blue eyes. "I can get that for ya, Alvin." She glanced at Dolfe. "If that's okay?"

Dolfe gave her a smile. "Thanks, Suz."

She nodded, turning away and heading for the bar.

Dolfe caught Alvin eyeing the waitress's pert behind and lifted an eyebrow.

"Hey, man. You're like a giant party pooper. If God didn't want men to ogle cute little behinds he would have made 'em flat and wide."

"I can't believe you're trying to make God your wing man."

Sparks shrugged.

"If I was you I'd learn to mind my own business, Alvin," Dolfe said as he stood up. He started to walk away and stopped, turning back as if he'd just thought of something. He pitched his voice low so the other patrons couldn't hear. "You don't know of anyone who might have wanted to kill Mr. White do you?"

Alvin blinked like a squirrel in headlights. "I

already told ya I've never seen the man before. How would I know if somebody had it out for him?"

"I just thought maybe someone else was upset about all the new people coming around."

Sparks's dark brown eyes went wide as he realized what Dolfe was implying. He lifted his hands again. "Hey, man. I got nothing against all these new folks. They can drink girly beer wherever they want. I was just makin' conversation. That's all."

Dolfe let his gaze stall on the man's fleshy face for a moment longer and then turned away, lifting a hand over his head by way of goodbye. "Thanks for all your help, Alvin. It was very illuminating."

Several of the other men in the bar fixed Alvin with hostile glares and Dolfe wanted to laugh. Clearly being helpful wasn't an esteemed pursuit in *Tyrese's Bar.*

3

*B*laise wandered over to the bar and sat down on a stool next to Dierdre. The other woman didn't even look up from the spot where her finger swirled through a ring of condensation. "How you holdin' up?" Blaise asked her.

Dierdre shrugged. "Okay. It's not like I was still in love with the man."

"No, but it's a shock."

Dierdre's finger continued circling the wet ring. A barely touched glass of dark soda sat nearby.

"You want something to drink, girlfriend?"

Blaise gave Suz a smile. "A glass of water. If you don't mind?"

Suz quickly filled a tall glass and handed it to Blaise, reaching to squeeze her hand in silent support before she glanced toward Dierdre. "How about you, honey? You want something else?"

Dierdre finally looked up and Blaise noted the red rimmed eyes that sparkled with unshed tears. She sniffled, shaking her head. "Just to go home. I don't suppose you can help me with that?"

Blaise and Suz shared a glance. "Sorry, honey." Suz patted her hand. "I'm sure it won't be much longer. I think they've talked to almost everybody. You spoke to the detective already, right?"

Dierdre nodded, glancing back down to the water ring as her finger reclaimed it.

"I served him," Suz said suddenly, her blue gaze tense. She shook her head. "I can't believe this happened here."

Blaise reached across the bar and hugged her friend. "It's sad," she said, glancing toward Dierdre. The woman didn't seem to even notice their conversation. She was lost in her own thoughts. "What was he drinking?"

"Just beer," Suz responded with a shrug.

"Did he seem okay?"

Suz grabbed a rag and started wiping down the already clean bar. She hated to sit still in the best of times and when she was stressed she could become almost hyper. "He was fidgety. IIis gaze kept sliding to the door as if he was expecting somebody."

"Me," Dierdre said, finally looking up at Suz. "I asked him to meet me here."

Suz nodded. "I'm so sorry."

"I wish I knew why he died. If it was something I caused..."

"Oh no," Suz gave Blaise a wide-eyed look. "It's not your fault, honey."

Blaise wasn't entirely sure about that. Nobody would be certain until Brita figured out what happened. But she couldn't stand to see an old friend in such pain. "I'm sure this had nothing to do with you, D. He was probably sick. Maybe he had a heart attack or something." Blaise knew as she said the words they weren't true. She'd seen the dried foam around Roger's mouth and the broken capillaries in the whites of his eyes. He'd been very sick before he died. Poisoning kind of sick. But ill-conceived as it was, her assurance seemed to make Dierdre feel better.

"He was a good man." She laughed softly. "To tell you the truth I was a little surprised when he agreed to meet me. We hadn't spoken in years."

"What did you tell him?" Blaise asked. When Dierdre looked a question Blaise clarified. "About why you wanted to meet?"

"Oh, well, I lied to you earlier. He actually asked me to meet him here. When I saw you I thought..." She sighed. "Let's just say my self-esteem has taken a hit over the years."

"You thought he was going to try to hurt you again? With me?" Blaise shook her head. "That's pretty twisted, D."

Dierdre shrugged. "Our distributor sells *Tyrese's* a lot of beer. I try to support our customers whenever I can so I suggested we meet here. I had no idea you even worked here."

"I can't believe you work for one of the local breweries." Blaise was genuinely surprised. She would never have pictured Dierdre as a beer aficionado.

"It's true. In fact, I was just promoted to *New Accounts*. It's an executive position." Dierdre smiled, clearly proud of the promotion.

"That's awesome," Blaise told her, and to her vast surprise she discovered she meant it. "I'm surprised we haven't run into each other here before."

"Me too. Did you just start?"

"Blaise has been working here a few months," Suz said, grinning at her friend. "I got her the job."

Shaking her head, Dierdre murmured. "Small world."

"What did Roger want to talk to you about?" Blaise realized she was being a bit of a pit bull on the subject, but she found it pretty interesting her two old friends would just show up where she worked, one of them dropping dead.

"To tell you the truth I have no idea. He was kind of secretive and I didn't ask a lot of questions. The timing was good for me. My divorce was recently finalized and I have no idea how to meet people. I've been a boring old housewife for six years and I'm really out of the loop on the whole dating thing."

"Roger is...was...a good looking man." Suz said gently. "I'm a bit surprised he was still single."

Dierdre's head shot up and she narrowed her gaze on Suz. "He told you that?"

Suz looked taken aback at Dierdre's tone. "No. I've been in this business a long time. I'm pretty good at reading people."

"What did you read from Roger," Blaise asked, curious. Her friend hadn't been lying. She was an excellent judge of people. In fact she was almost psychic.

"I'd say he'd been worried about something. Like I said before, he was jumpy. But it was more than that. He had circles under his eyes and his color wasn't good. His clothes hung on him like he'd recently lost a lot of weight. And he had no tan line on his ring finger so if he was married he didn't wear the ring."

"Sounds like whatever he was worried about might have caught up with him," Blaise said aloud before she realized her mistake. She wanted to kick herself when Dierdre's shocked gaze slid to hers.

"You think he was murdered?" She fairly shouted the question, causing all eyes in the bar to swing her way.

Blaise threw an apologetic glance in Brita's direction.

The cop was questioning the beer delivery kid across the bar.

"I just meant that maybe it caused him to have a heart attack or something."

"He was a little young for a heart attack, don't you think?" Dierdre asked coolly.

Blaise didn't respond. She figured she'd said quite enough for the moment.

Fortunately, Suz had no such compunction. "I'm sure Roger was looking forward to seeing you again."

Dierdre didn't look all that sure. "Actually, when he first called he seemed eager to get off the phone. But then we got talking about our lives. Family and friends we hadn't seen in a while, jobs and stuff, and he seemed to get more comfortable."

"What kind of job did Roger have?" Blaise asked.

"He works...worked...for an independent testing lab."

Blaise grinned. "Really? I always thought he'd be a big Wall Street tycoon or something."

"I know, right?" Dierdre shared the smile.

"Ladies and gentlemen!"

They turned at the sound of Brita's voice. "You can all leave now. I have your contact information and I'll have to ask that you don't travel out of Indianapolis for the time being. In case I have more questions for you."

Dierdre sighed. Grabbing her purse off the back of her stool she turned to Blaise. "It was nice seeing you again, B. I'm sorry it was under such horrible circumstances."

Blaise gave in to an impulse and pulled the other woman into a hug. "I hope we'll see you again. Drinks are on me next time."

Dierdre's eyes momentarily lost their haunted look. "I'd like that a lot." She waved toward Suz and started out of the bar.

Watching her shuffle sadly toward the door, Blaise couldn't help wondering what had really inspired her old friend to meet with Roger White again after so long. Because she didn't believe for a second it was a clumsy ploy for romance.

"B?" Suz grinned up at Blaise. "Like Aunt Bee?"

"It's just a thing from High School." She shrugged. "But I can see why you'd mistake me for Aunt Bee. We're a lot alike."

Suz blew a queen sized raspberry. "As if."

"You ready to go home, Beautiful?"

Blaise swung around to find Dolfe striding in her direction. Brita was with him. "Home? Is the bar closing?"

"It's a crime scene now," Brita said.

Blaise and Suz shared a look. Then Suz glanced across the bar to the spot where Tyrese sat, looking worried. "Ty's gonna have kittens."

Brita shrugged. "It can't be helped. There's a really good chance that Roger White was poisoned in this bar. My people need to go over everything and see if we can find what he was poisoned with and how."

"Oh my god!" Suz went pale. "What if somebody else gets sick?"

Blaise realized her friend had misunderstood Brita's statement but she didn't clarify it for her. Thinking somebody had gotten a bad case of food poisoning was bad enough, if Suz realized Brita was saying he was murdered she'd be the one having kittens, or full grown cats. "I'm sure it'll be fine. Tyrese works too hard anyway. He can use a night off."

Suz frowned but nodded. "I'll just finish cleaning up."

Brita reached out and touched Suz on the arm. "Just leave it, please. We need to see everything as it is now."

Suz's frown deepened but she nodded. "I'll see you later, B." She grinned and gave Blaise a hug. "Talk to you in the morning?"

"Absolutely. Enjoy your night off." Blaise watched Suz go over to Tyrese and drop an arm around his shoulders. She leaned down and spoke into his ear, earning a half smile from the despondent owner. Not for the first time, Blaise wondered what relationship the two of them shared. They seemed very close. Closer than just friends, which was what they both kept insisting they were to each other.

Dolfe wrapped a strong arm around her waist. "Let's go home, future wife. I have some ideas for how to fill up your night."

Brita covered her ears. "Stop right there. I don't want to hear details."

Blaise laughed. "Now why do you think we're going to give you details?"

"Because ever since I made the mistake of letting you two know it bothers me, you never miss a chance."

Dolfe winked at Blaise. Leaning closer, he spoke softly enough for only Brita to hear. "The first thing I intend to do is run a hot bubble bath…"

Brita elbowed him in the hard expanse of his gut and he danced away, laughing.

"Then I'll probably light some candles…" Blaise added.

"La, la, la, la, la…"

"And I'll pour us both a glass of wine," Dolfe said, snagging Brita around the shoulders and pulling her close so he could speak in her ear.

She tried to wrench away but he just laughed. "And then I'm going to break out the nail polish…"

Brita's eyes went wide. "You wouldn't!"

"Oh, he would," Blaise giggled. "Fire engine red."

"Ah…lalalalalalalalalala!" Brita sang in desperation.

Dolfe kissed Brita on the forehead. "Okay, you big weenie. You win. Tell Percy I said hey."

Blaise grinned at her friend. "I can't believe you're a big, strong cop and you're afraid of a few painted toes."

Brita grimaced. "Not just the toes. The entire human foot appalls me."

Blaise patted her on the shoulder. "There's probably therapy for that."

"Yeah," Brita groused. "The therapy is to get new friends who don't discuss their feet every five minutes."

4

*D*olfe had just finished the final coat of *Rattlin' Red* polish on Blaise's right big toe when he gave a heartfelt exclamation, "Oh, crap!"

She was lying back in the big tub with bubbles tickling her nose. Dolfe's strong hands were caressing her feet and she was deep in a blissful moment. Opening one eye, Blaise offered up a heartfelt prayer that he wouldn't stop. "What's wrong?"

"Oh, I promised that delivery kid I'd call his boss and clear his being late on his deliveries."

She opened the other eye. "And why is that your job?"

He shrugged, grinning. "You disappoint me, grasshopper. If I didn't call, I wouldn't get a chance to quiz the guy about what he knows."

She sat up, taking care to keep her freshly

painted foot out of the water. "You think he's involved in the murder?"

"It's too soon to tell..." Dolfe ran a big, warm finger along her shin. "But Roger White was poisoned in a bar and *OnPoint Distributors* supplied some of the things a guy could get poisoned with. It makes sense to at least rule them out."

She closed her eyes again and leaned back as Dolfe's fingers found her calf and returned to kneading it. "Mmmm, okay."

Dolfe lowered her leg and pushed to his feet. Blaise's eyes snapped open. "Where are you going?"

He grinned down at her, a perfect glistening statue of hard, soapy male. "To make the phone call."

Her eyes went wide. "Oh no you don't!" She shoved to her feet, skidded on the bottom of the tub and squealed as she fell forward into his arms.

Dolfe caught her, his hands sliding as she bounced hard against his chest. He sucked in a surprised breath and threw his arms around her before she slipped off and fell. "Be careful, Beautiful."

Blaise wrapped herself around his warm, slippery hardness and nearly purred as her body leapt to life. "The phone call can wait. You have a future wife who needs you right now."

He placed his sexy mouth on hers, giving her a

soft, lingering kiss. When he broke the kiss he smiled. "Greedy woman."

She danced her fingers over his hard pecs, down the rippled wonder of his firm belly, and lower still...

Dolfe gasped, his eyes going wide.

"You can't just paint a woman's nails and then walk away," she told him in a slightly breathless voice. Her hand skimmed over silky hardness, drawing a long, heartfelt groan from him.

"I'm starting to see your point," Dolfe said on a growl.

"Good," Blaise grinned. "Because I can definitely see yours."

Nathan Lord's boss's name was Pete Galgorn. His office hours on the card Nathan gave Dolfe were ten to eight Monday through Saturday. Dolfe hoped the guy made a good living doing what he did, because his hours were almost as bad as Dolfe's.

He dialed the number despite the fact that it was nearly nine thirty at night. Dolfe figured with *OnPoint Distributors* out delivering product until late evening hours, Galgorn might be available by phone after hours.

His assumption was proven right when Galgorn answered his phone after five rings. "Yeah."

"Mr. Galgorn?"

"This is my phone so yeah, I assume it's me."

Dolfe smiled to himself. Nathan hadn't been exaggerating. His boss was a total grouch. "I'm glad I caught you, sir. My name is Dolfe Honeybun and I'm working with IMPD on a suspicious death investigation."

"What does that have to do with me?"

"I spoke to your employee, Nathan Lord tonight at *Tyrese's Bar*."

"You think Nathan killed somebody? That's just great. Now I have to hire a new guy. I don't have time for this shit."

"Mr. Galgorn, as far as I know Nathan didn't kill anybody. But he was retained with the rest of the customers at *Tyrese's* while the detective in charge questioned everybody."

"Okay, I get it. This is one of Nate's friends, calling to cover for him because he was late with his deliveries again isn't it? I mean...Honeybun? Really? You guys can do better than that. Oh, wait. Are you trying to be ironic?"

That one gave Dolfe brief pause. He shook his head. "I assure you the name is real. In fact, dozens of Honeybun men and women have been using it without discernible problems for our entire lives."

Galgorn snorted. "You think I'm buying this? Which one of you punk ass kids is this?"

"Sir, do I sound like a twenty-something kid?"

"No. But you might of gotten that husky voice from smokin' too many fags. My gramma smoked two packs a day for twenty years. If you didn't see her you'd think she was a longshoreman from Jersey."

"I'm sure your gramma was a wonderful woman with the patience of a saint. If you'd like I can stop by and show you my investigator's license."

Galgorn expelled air. "That won't be necessary. What can I help you with, Mr. Honeybee?"

Dolfe didn't bother to correct him. It was clear the man was just trying to get his goat. "A man was poisoned at Tyrese's tonight. I'm following up to find out if you've had any problems with the microbreweries you work with? Any hint of bad beer? Inventory you've had to return?"

"Not a whisper. If we had we'd isolate and deal with the problem right away. We take quality control very personally, Honeybee. If something happens we're the first ones on the hot seat."

"What do you know about *Artisan Beers*?"

There was a very brief, almost indiscernible pause before Galgorn spoke. "Good beer. We distribute a lot of it."

"You've never had any issues with their quality?"

"If I had I wouldn't still be distributing the beer. Some of these new breweries try to pass off skunk beer caused by bargain hops or poor temperature control. I don't do business with those amateurs again. As far as I know *Artisan's* top notch."

Galgorn's careful, almost civil tone made Dolfe think he was hiding something. He decided to dig a bit deeper. "What about the owner, the personnel. Any issues there?"

"Art Sands is a great guy. A man's man. He keeps a low profile though, lets that Kopper fella run things."

"No money problems?"

"How the hell would I know? Do I look like an accountant to you?"

"Actually you currently look like a cell phone." Dolfe quipped. "But I was referring to their timeliness in paying *OnPoint*."

"I'd have to check my records to be sure but as far as I know they've never been late." A female voice mumbled something in the background and Galgorn covered the mouthpiece to respond. "I got to go, Honeybee. If you need anything else from me get a warrant." He hung up without waiting for Dolfe to respond.

Dolfe disconnected and glanced at his watch, wondering if it was too late to call *Artisan Beers*.

*A*rtisan *Beers* was located in a narrow red brick building on the outskirts of Indianapolis. Its northwestern location was handy to the bars on and near the high energy area of Broad Ripple Village.

Dolfe realized he'd driven past the building a hundred times and wondered if it had always been a microbrewery. "David Kopper said he'd be in by eight."

Blaise nodded, her head bobbing to a song on the radio. "It was nice of him to meet you so early."

Dolfe lifted an eyebrow. "If somebody hadn't distracted me last night, I could have just done it by phone."

She grinned, unrepentant. "This will be more fun anyway. I've never toured a microbrewery."

He pulled into a small lot at the side of the building. "I don't think there's much to see. Just a bunch of big metal containers with nozzles."

He parked his truck and climbed out, walking around to give Blaise a hand down. She pretended to fall into him as her feet hit the ground and he grabbed her, grinning as she pressed herself against him.

"Oopsies."

"Yeah, I got your oopsies. You're a she-devil, you know that?"

"Do I have you under my spell?"

He kissed the end of her dainty nose. "I think you already know the answer to that."

"I do," she linked her arm through his. "But I still want to hear you say it."

He pulled the door open and a bell jangled, announcing their arrival. Inside the brightly lit lobby, a veritable forest of vibrant, green plants dominated. Beyond the verdant display, a wall of windows showed off an army of stainless steel tanks, lined up like tin soldiers.

A tall, forty-something-year-old woman entered from a door at the side of the lobby. She smiled when she saw them, extending a hand as she approached. "Good morning! Are you here for a tour?" The woman had a movie star voice, with a deep, sexy timbre that was totally at odds with her sour expression.

Dolfe took her hand, finding his fingers unceremoniously squeezed. "I'm Dolfe Honeybun. I had an appointment with Mr. Kopper."

"Ah, yes. He mentioned you were coming." She shook her head. "Can I ask what this is about?"

"I'm sorry, I'm not at liberty to disclose that. If I could just speak to Mr. Kopper?"

She stared at him for a moment, clearly unhappy to be excluded. Anger flashed through her gaze and disappeared almost immediately. She gave him a tight smile. "Of course. Let me just give him a call and let him know you're here." She moved stiffly toward a glass and metal desk in the corner and picked up the phone, punching a button and speaking into it. A moment later she returned. "If you'll just follow me."

David Kopper was not at all what Dolfe had expected. He had bright red hair that flared around his long, pale face in tight coils. He was also very tall, close to Dolfe's six foot five inches in fact, but gangly rather than muscular. However, when he gripped Dolfe's hand he squeezed, showing an unexpected amount of strength.

"It's a pleasure to meet you, Mr. Honeybun. I've actually been thinking about hiring a private investigator so this is fortuitous."

Dolfe let one eyebrow peak with interest. "Oh? What kind of service are you looking for?"

The man shook his head. "We can get into that another time. In the meantime..." He turned a predatory smile toward Blaise. "Please introduce me to your delightful assistant."

Blaise's usual good humor paled as he reached for her hand, capturing it between both of his. Dolfe gave a moment's thought to rescuing the clueless businessman, and then decided he didn't deserve it.

Blaise quickly extricated her hand from his grip. "My name's Blaise, Mr. Kopper, but you can call me Miss Runa because I can tell by the way you're looking at me how much you respect me as a person."

Kopper blinked in surprise and then let his oily smile slide away. "Yes. Well." He turned to Dolfe. "What can I help you with, Mr. Honeybun?"

"Are you aware of the incident at *Tyrese's Bar* last night?"

Kopper's long face folded into a frown. "I'm not. What happened?"

"A man was poisoned and died." Blaise told him. "He was drinking one of your beers."

Kopper walked around his desk, head down to hide his expression.

Dolfe almost smiled. If Kopper thought a hunk of glass and metal would save him from Blaise's ire he was sadly mistaken.

"Are you implying he was poisoned by our beer? That's ludicrous." Kopper leaned back in an uncomfortable looking white leather chair. "We regularly test our beer, Mr. Honeybun, both internally and externally for an extra measure of quality control. If there's even the slightest problem with a batch we destroy the entire lot."

"Is it possible you made a mistake?" Dolfe asked. "It happens."

"Or maybe you thought you could slip something by just once," Blaise said.

"What a brilliant PR move that would be, eh?" Kopper asked on a bitter laugh. "I can see the slogan now. 'Buy our beers and die happy.'" He stood. "If that's all..."

"There's just one more thing." Dolfe avoided Blaise's gaze when it swung his way. It was slightly possible she wasn't going to like what she was about to hear. "Are you familiar with a woman named Dierdre Masterson?"

Blaise's hostile glare burned the side of his face but he managed not to glance her way.

"Do you think Dierdre killed that man?" Kopper didn't even bother to try to hide his surprise.

"Please just answer the question, sir."

"Well of course I know her. The microbrewery world is a small one. She works at *Byerson's Beers.* Smart woman. Good at what she does. I've tried to steal her away from Alex Byerson, myself. Unfortunately she doesn't seem inclined to make the change."

Dolfe glanced at Blaise just to see her reaction. Finally, a woman Kopper seemed to respect.

"Why do you ask?"

"She knew the victim. Had an appointment with him there. I just wondered if you might have known what she could have been there to discuss with him."

"What was the man's name?"

"Roger White," Blaise said, skimming a hostile glance Dolfe's way.

Kopper paled, his smallish blue eyes bobbling nervously around the room. "Nope. Sorry. Now if you'll excuse me..." He pushed upright as if by standing he could force them to leave.

"Mr. Kopper..." Dolfe warned.

The other man finally caught Dolfe's gaze and held it for a beat before looking away. He sighed, dropping heavily into his ugly chair. "White was with *Clear Brew Laboratories*. He didn't like anything we sent him last month. It was brutal. We ended up dumping two batches of beer. Do you have any idea how expensive that is?"

"What was the problem?"

"He claimed the equipment wasn't cleaned properly and the beer was tainted. If you ask me it was all trumped up. The man's a nutcase. He's one of those beer purists. Personally I think he just does it to scare the microbreweries into testing more stock. Whatever the reason, the owner of *Artisan* fell for it and I'll have trouble paying the bills next month."

Dolfe stared hard at the man for a moment and then quietly asked. "Mr. Kopper, where were you at seven-thirty last night?"

Kopper's head snapped up. "You don't seriously think...?"

"Just answer the question, sir."

Kopper expelled a shaky breath. Even Blaise stopped glowering at him as her pretty face softened with pity.

"I can't tell you that. Not right now anyway."

"Why not?"

Kopper swore softly, his long fingers digging angrily through the fiery nest of his hair.

"Mr. Kopper?"

"Because if I do I might be the next one on the killer's list!"

5

"*How* ow the heck can he just lay that on us and then not tell us what's going on?" Blaise had her hands clenched in angry fists on her knees and her fiery gaze locked blindly on the world beyond the windshield.

Dolfe frowned. "It's pretty frustrating. I'll tell Brita about our conversation with Mr. Kopper. Maybe she'll be able to get him to talk."

"We should have gotten tougher with him."

Dolfe let an eyebrow climb skyward. "And what...torture him into full disclosure?"

She seemed to be considering it. "Maybe just a teensy bit of water boarding."

He chuckled. "With a doily and a shot glass?"

Grinning widely, Blaise seemed to regain her good humor. It was one of the things he loved about her. She was a passionate woman, prone to fits of temper. But she just as easily dumped anger in favor of humor or passion. "I'm starving."

Or other things.

He nodded. "Sit down or drive through?"

"Pancake palace. I'm in the mood for a double stack of blueberry waffles."

"You got it, Princess."

She smacked him on the arm. "You know I hate it when you call me that."

"If the glass shoe fits..."

A black sedan sped past going the opposite direction, a pale face with wide eyes behind the driver's side window. Dolfe threw on the brakes and pulled a quick U-turn to the accompaniment of multiple horns.

Blaise grabbed the dash. "What the...?"

"Looks like you're going to have to wait for that waffle, Beautiful."

"A car chase! Sweet!" She happily checked her seat belt and then gripped the panic handle in the ceiling. "Who are we chasing?"

The sedan ahead took a right turn so quickly the back tires slipped out from underneath it for a couple of beats before the driver managed to get the car under control. The delay allowed Dolfe to close the gap a bit. By the time he made the turn he was only a couple of cars away from the sedan.

As the sedan careened around another corner he noticed something that made his blood run cold.

Another car took the turn right on its bumper, accelerating into the turn as the driver fought to keep control.

He watched in horror as the black sedan side-swiped a parked car and shot across two lanes of traffic. A car coming from the opposite direction smashed into the back of it, sending it spinning until it crashed into a hard landing against a lamp post.

"Yikes," Blaise breathed. "I hope they're all right."

Dolfe slammed his foot down on the accelerator as the chase car pulled up next to the sedan and a window rolled down. He realized with a horrified flash of instinct what was about to happen. A beat later he was proven right as a gun emerged from the window.

"Crap! Down, Blaise."

He hit the horn and veered directly for the gunman's car, the gas pedal slammed to the floor.

His pulse roaring in his head, Dolfe was only barely aware of Blaise's muttered, "woof" as he played a terrifying game of chicken, praying the other guy would call it quits before Dolfe did.

At the last possible moment the driver of the chase car accelerated out of Dolfe's path and sped off. He slammed his foot down on the brake, suddenly fearful he'd be the one to kill the unfortunate driver of the sedan, and spared a quick glance at the low-slung muscle car speeding away from them.

The big truck's tires squealed, leaving rubber across the road leading to the still immobile sedan. Dolfe eased to a stop a foot away from the black car. He glanced quickly at Blaise and found her wide-eyed but seemingly unharmed. "You okay?"

"Yeah, but..."

He couldn't wait for her questions. Dolfe opened the truck door and leapt out, running toward the sedan. He tried the door and found it locked. Pounding on the glass, he bent down and peered inside.

Dierdre Masterson lay half across the middle console, her face bloody and one arm twisted at an odd angle from the crash. The airbag had deployed, its used up carcass sagging from the steering wheel.

She wasn't moving.

He pounded on the glass again. "Dierdre! Wake up. I need you to unlock the door."

Nothing.

"Here, buddy. Let me get it."

A clean cut young man approached him with a long piece of metal. "I'm a fireman. I can open the door."

Dolfe slapped him on the arm. "Good. Thanks."

A moment later the door was open and Dolfe sent the fireman to call an ambulance. Then he leaned inside and pushed Dierdre's hair off her face.

The brown strands stuck in the blood painting her cheek as he tucked it back. "Dierdre? Are you awake?"

"Is she all right?" Blaise's breathless question came from just behind him.

"Dierdre?" Dolfe put two fingers on her throat. "Weak pulse." He turned his head and repeated his request for an ambulance in a shout.

He felt Blaise's soft, firm grip on his arm. "Dolfe?"

Dierdre's arm twitched beneath his hand. "She's waking up. Dierdre? Take it easy. You've been in an accident."

The woman's eyes fluttered open and she groaned. Slowly, with Dolfe's help, she eased upright. Then, her eyes wild with fear, she gripped his arm. "You have to help. They're trying to kill me."

Dolfe glanced up as sirens screamed closer. "You're safe. Just keep still until the ambulance gets here."

She shook her head, her eyes wide. Spotting Blaise through the window she implored her. "B, tell him. I have to hide. If they find me I'm dead."

Blaise put her hand on Dolfe's back and he moved aside. Crouching beside the car, she clasped one of Dierdre's hands in her own. "Nobody's going to hurt you now, D. You're safe."

Blaise's friend kept shaking her head, her eyes wide and dancing constantly around as if she expected the driver of the muscle car to emerge from the shadows.

"Step aside, please."

Dolfe grabbed Blaise's hand and pulled her away as the EMTs rolled a gurney up and bent to examine Dierdre.

"She's terrified, Dolfe."

"From what I saw she has a right to be. She's right. Whoever was driving that car was trying to kill her." He nodded toward the back and sides of her car, where bullets had dented and torn the glossy finish. "They weren't just trying to run her off the road. This was more than a warning."

"This has to be tied to Roger's killing," Blaise said, frowning.

"Yeah. Which means there's something she hasn't told us."

Two EMTs, a burly guy and a small but muscular woman, got Dierdre onto the gurney and lifted it. Dolfe moved closer. "Dierdre, you need to tell us what's going on or we can't help you."

"I don't know! I swear."

"You told us the truth about your meeting with Roger at Tyrese's?"

The woman bit her lip, her gaze sliding toward Blaise. Finally, she sighed. "Okay, I lied a little bit. Roger called me because he said he'd discovered something and he wanted my opinion about what he should do. He made me promise not to tell anybody why we were meeting so I made up the renewing a romance story. I figured it would be fine. Why would anybody think otherwise?"

"Somebody thinks otherwise, D," Blaise told her old friend. "They just tried to kill you."

Tears shimmered in Dierdre's gaze and she sniffled. "I know. I'm terrified. First Roger and now..." Shaking her head, she burst into tears.

"We need to get her to the hospital," the female EMT told Dolfe.

He nodded. "Thanks."

Blaise grasped her friend's hand. "We'll meet you at the hospital."

"No!" Dierdre shook her head. "If they see me talking to you..."

"You're in danger, Miss Masterson. You need to trust us," Dolfe told her.

She was still shaking her head as they rolled her toward the ambulance.

"What are we going to do, babe?" Blaise asked him. "She's scared out of her mind and if she won't let us help..."

"I'm calling Brita. She needs to put a cop on Dierdre's door at the hospital until we figure out what's going on."

Blaise nodded, looking relieved.

Brita answered on the third ring, sounding harried. "Hey, Dolfe."

"We just witnessed an attempt on Dierdre Masterson's life."

A long, weary sigh sounded on the other end. "Tell me."

He filled her in on everything that had happened that morning, including their interview with Kopper.

"Okay. You're right. They're not telling us everything. I'll talk to them both. In the meantime, will you do me a favor?"

"Sure, what do you need?"

"I'm up to my eyeballs in murders. My caseload's tripled since yesterday. Could you do some of the legwork on the White case for me? Since Blaise knows some of the players you might get farther than I could."

"Absolutely. I was thinking we should talk to Roger White's boss. See what client tests he was working on, just in case we're barking up the wrong tree with this brewery angle."

"Makes sense. Just keep me posted, k?"

"You got it." He hung up and looked at Blaise. She was staring off after the retreating ambulance, a speculative gleam in her pretty brown eyes. He tucked a fingertip under her delicate jaw and lifted her face so he could give her a long, tender kiss. As he broke the kiss, he sighed. "I feel better now."

Her lush lips curved up in the corners. "Funny, I feel all hot and bothered."

Slinging an arm around her shoulders, Dolfe led her back to his truck. "Brita wants us to talk to Roger's boss. You up for another interview?"

"Of course! But you need to feed me first." She waggled slender black brows. "I'm famished."

He couldn't help chuckling. "You're always famished."

"A woman with less confidence than me might take that as an insult."

"Then I'm not worried at all about how you're going to take it. You have more confidence than a middle-aged man fresh out of a divorce."

"Dang!" she told him. "It's a good thing I'm not sensitive. I might have folded into the fetal position on that one."

He was laughing as he circled around to the driver's side.

Her belly full of blueberry waffles, Blaise was looking forward to the interview. She'd never visited a beer testing lab and was excited about it. In her imagination the place was filled with belching scientists wearing rumpled lab coats and declaring their test subjects delicate, with a fruity finish or bold and woody with a meaty froth.

The gray stone building where the lab was

located had charcoal tinted windows and copper colored finishes. The doors swung open as they approached and two people in lab coats, a man and a woman, emerged, chatting amiably.

The office building where *Clear Brew Testing Laboratories* was located was near the center of town. The lobby of the big building was spacious, cool, and starkly modern. Blaise glanced around as Dolfe read a sign on the wall.

"Second floor," he told her.

She eyed the bricked-in atrium garden beyond double glass doors across the lobby and the upscale restaurant to their right. "Beer testing must be lucrative," she told Dolfe archly as they headed for the elevators.

He punched the *Up* arrow. "Especially if every test is done multiple times," he said thoughtfully.

"Are you thinking they're scamming these microbreweries?"

"Not necessarily. But from what I've read, a lot of these breweries are started by people with minimal experience in brewing. Sometimes all they've done is home brew before they take the plunge. I'm sure these startups make a lot of mistakes and have multiple failures before they get their beer up to snuff."

Nodding, Blaise punched the button for the second floor. "If dumping batches and retesting is threatening the livelihood of an established company like *Artisan Beers*, I can't even imagine what it would do to a relatively new company."

"Exactly," Dolfe agreed. "Sounds like a lot of potential motives for murder."

Blaise sighed. She'd liked Roger when they were friends. He'd been a nice guy who'd helped her through some pretty normal but still painful situations growing up. She hated to think of him as the guy everybody loves to hate, but that was certainly shaping up to be the most likely cause of his murder. "Hopefully his boss can tell us something that will help us narrow down the suspect pool."

The lab's name was splashed across a glass wall in large, copper colored letters, the font swirly and feminine instead of the heavy block letters Blaise expected for a scientific business. It was one of the reasons...the other being the throw pillows in the lobby...that Blaise wasn't surprised when the receptionist escorted them into the owner's office and a young, attractive woman stood to greet them.

"Good morning," she said with a smile. Stepping out from behind a light ash and chrome desk, the pretty blonde offered Blaise her hand. "I'm Tabitha Clear. I own *Clear Brew Labs*."

The woman's hand was soft, her nails neatly manicured and coated with cotton candy pink polish. Blaise accepted the handshake, noting the woman's business-like chignon and the form fitting dark suit. Tabitha Clear might be young, probably no older than thirty, but she did a good job of looking and acting professional.

"It's nice to meet you. I'm Blaise Runa and this is my fiancé, Dolfe Honeybun."

Tabitha smiled widely as she shook his hand. "Congratulations! When's the wedding?"

Dolfe skimmed Blaise a glance, his dark blond brows lifting. "I'll be the last to know, I think. When are we getting married, again?"

She narrowed her gaze at her smart-mouthed boyfriend. "I'm not sure. We'll get to it eventually."

Tabitha laughed airily. "A free spirit, I love it." She indicated the chairs in front of her desk. "Please sit. Tell me what I can do to help." She shook her head as she returned to her chair. "I have to admit, I know most of the names in this business and I'm not familiar with yours. Are you a startup?"

It took Blaise a beat to realize the woman's misconception. She opened her mouth to clarify but Dolfe beat her to it.

He flashed his investigator's license. "Actually, we're here about the death of your employee, Roger White."

Tabitha's pretty face folded into a frown. She even managed to add a tear-like shimmer to her blue gaze. "Of course. I should have guessed. You think there was foul play?"

If Dolfe was surprised by her question he didn't give any indication. Blaise felt it like a punch to her gut. The manufactured tears didn't fool Blaise. Tabitha Clear was practiced, careful, and cold enough to freeze rubber. She'd clearly been expecting someone to come around asking questions.

"We believe he was poisoned."

"Oh my!" She placed her perfect hand in the center of her chest, where a heart should have been beating. Blaise doubted there was anything under there aside from a block of ice. Tabitha lowered her head, sniffling delicately. "That's terrible." She looked up a moment later, dry eyed and serious. "I'm not sure what you think I can tell you about that."

"I'd like to see his recent client reports. Check out his findings."

The blue gaze widened appropriately. "You think one of our clients killed him?"

"It's a possibility we need to rule out."

Blaise sat forward, giving the woman a supportive smile. "It's horrible isn't it? I was a friend of Roger's, though we hadn't seen each other in years."

Tabitha's gaze grew calculating. "You knew him? Oh, I'm so sorry for your loss." She reached across her desk and patted Blaise's hand. "I really liked Roger. Everybody did."

"That's not the story we've been hearing," Dolfe told her. "In fact, I understand some of your clients were unhappy with him."

Blaise watched the woman carefully and saw the spark of anger and something else that looked like worry cross her features. "Whoever told you that was lying, Detective..."

"Just Dolfe, I'm in the private sector."

"Dolfe. Occasionally someone would be upset about a finding. Of course they would be. The tests aren't horribly expensive but there are many variables in brewing a great beer and testing does add up. If we find issues the breweries are faced with the need to dump batches of their beer. That's an expensive proposition."

"I'm surprised they put themselves through that," Blaise said carefully.

Tabitha looked truly shocked. "Well of course they do. It only takes one bad experience to ruin a microbrewery. Reputation is everything when you're small and just starting out."

"Can you think of anyone else who might have wanted Roger dead?"

"Not really. I don't know much about his personal life. Roger was very private."

"How about other employees?"

"Oh no, my people are very close. They develop a sort of 'us against the world' mentality, I'm afraid. That kind of climate doesn't support backstabbing."

"There's nobody who might have thought Roger's absence would make his or her career options brighter?"

Amazingly the woman laughed. "You've been watching too much TV, Det...er...Dolfe. There's none of that. I pay my employees very well and they love their jobs." She punched an intercom button and called the receptionist back. "Ginny will show you to Roger's station. Please feel free to look at whatever you'd like. But I can't let you take anything out of the office. My clients' information is private and confidential."

Following the petite receptionist at a bit of a distance, Blaise leaned close and whispered to Dolfe. "She was awfully easy about us looking at Roger's stuff."

"Yeah. Which tells me she knows there's nothing there. We'll go through the motions though."

Ginny stopped beside a door and motioned them inside. "This is...was...Roger's office." She tucked a chin-length strand of straight dark hair behind her ear and eased a hungry look over Dolfe. "Can I get you anything?" Her brown eyes widened just enough to make Blaise want to accidentally bash her with her bag as she passed by. Instead she stepped between them and smiled. "I love your hair. Where do you get it cut?"

The woman tried to peer over Blaise's right shoulder just as Dolfe ducked into Roger's office on the left.

"Um, okay then," Ginny said, ignoring Blaise as

she called out to Dolfe. "I'll be right here if you need me."

"You probably have work to do," he told her with a smile that made the poor woman's mouth drop open with unadulterated lust. "We'll just be a few minutes. I'll stop by the front desk on my way out to let you know we're done."

Ginny gulped, her slender throat convulsing as if she'd accidently swallowed a toad. "I um...I'm supposed to stay and...erm...watch." She batted her eyelashes apologetically.

Dolfe nodded. "Okay then, we'll try to be fast."

"Don't hurry on my account." Ginny's lashes fluttered again and Blaise had to clasp her hands together to keep from whacking the woman upside the head. She turned away and joined Dolfe in the tiny lab slash office. He sat down in front of the computer and looked up at her, his sexy green gaze sliding to her oversized bag.

Blaise settled her bag on the edge of the desk and turned, throwing Ginny a smile. "I wonder if you could show me where I might get some coffee. I ate one too many waffles and I'm getting sleepy."

Ginny frowned, skimming a reluctant glance toward Dolfe and then nodded. "The break room's just down the hall. We have those little coffee pods."

Blaise fell into step beside her, nodding enthusiastically. "Oh! I love those! You can pick whatever kind of coffee you want and it's always perfect."

Ginny grinned. "Right? We have several flavors and just plain old black for the non-adventurous among us."

Blaise laughed gaily. "That would be my Dolfe. He drinks his like tar."

The room looked like any other break room. It was small, probably only twelve feet by twelve feet, with a round table in the center. The wall across from the door was covered in cabinets, both upper and lower, with a counter that ran from wall to wall. In the center of that counter was a stainless steel sink. A microwave oven sat on the counter next to the coffee machine and beside it was a basket filled with popcorn packets.

Blaise let her eyes go wide. "Popcorn! My own, personal crack. Do you mind if I make some?"

Ginny threw a worried glance toward the door and then smiled. "Sure. I thought you said you were full, though."

"Full? Good heavens, woman! I'm never full. I can eat almost around the clock."

Ginny eyed Blaise's tall, lean form and sighed. "It must be awesome to be tall. You can eat anything and you look amazing in clothes."

"Why thank you, girlfriend." Blaise gave the other woman an impulsive hug. "That's really nice of you to say. But you know, men love petite women too. You make them feel all caveman-ish."

She giggled. "I'm sorry about before."

Blaise stuck a bag of popcorn into the microwave and punched some buttons. "About what?"

"Ogling your man. That was rude of me."

Blaise shrugged. "He's pretty stupendous. It happens a lot."

Leaning a hip against the counter, Ginny cocked her head and asked, "How can you stand it? I'd go batshit crazy."

"I used to. But I know Dolfe loves me so I've learned to just be proud of him." The microwave dinged and Blaise pulled out the bag. "Tell you the truth, I wake up every morning and wonder what he could possibly see in me. I'm in awe that he loves me." She shrugged, tugging on the corners of the bag to open it.

"You make a gorgeous couple."

"Aw..." Blaise's eyes teared up and she hugged Ginny again. She offered the receptionist the popcorn and Ginny pinched a few kernels out of the bag.

They crunched in silence for a minute. Ginny finally looked up into Blaise's eyes. "You're investigating Roger's death, aren't you?"

"Yeah." Blaise felt a wave of unexpected sadness. "He was my friend. We went to high school together."

"Really! Oh, I didn't know. I'm sorry."

Blaise nodded. "Did you know him very well?"

"Not well. He was kind of quiet. Kept to himself. But I liked him. He seemed like a nice guy."

"He was." Blaise shook her head. "I really wish we could figure out who might want him dead."

Ginny bit her lip, staring at the floor for a beat. It was enough for Blaise's antennae to go up. "What is it? Did you think of something?"

Ginny glanced out the door. "No. I mean. Maybe. It's just..."

Blaise grabbed her hand and tugged her more deeply into the room, away from the door. "Tell me. I won't let anybody know you told."

Ginny's teeth worried her lip for anther moment and then she leaned close, speaking softly. "He fought with Tabitha the other night. They were screaming about something. It was after everybody else had left and I was getting my stuff together to go too. They were walking out together and they stopped just up the hall from the lobby."

"Did you hear what they were fighting about," Blaise asked.

"Not really. Roger just kept insisting Tab had to let him do the right thing but she told him to stay out of it. That she'd take care of things."

"Then what?"

Ginny shook her head. "I got out of here before they saw me. I didn't want to...er...embarrass them."

Blaise patted her new friend's arm. "Thanks for telling me."

Ginny looked relieved. "I'm sure it wasn't anything important. Sometimes they argue about the right way to break bad news to clients. Tab likes to give it to them straight on, like pulling off a band aid she says. But Roger feels...felt...bad." She paled as she seemed to remember he was gone. "He tried to deliver his own reports but Tab would go behind his back sometimes."

"Why do you suppose she did that?"

Ginny shrugged. "They're very competitive with each other...or were. Roger was the first lab tech she hired after she opened the business and apparently he owned a significant number of shares."

Blaise nodded, thinking that if Tabitha ever wanted full control so she could sell the business those shares that Roger owned might be a problem for her. "Thanks so much. It was good to talk to you about Roger. It makes me feel better to know I was right about him all those years ago."

Ginny nodded. "I should probably get back. If Tab finds out I left your boyfriend alone in there..."

Blaise patted her hand, setting the mostly uneaten popcorn onto the table. "Let's go. I don't want you to get into trouble."

6

*D*olfe met the two women at the door to Roger White's office. He handed Blaise her purse, thanked Ginny and ushered Blaise toward the exit. As he pushed her gently through the door she balked, throwing up her hands. "Slow down, future hubby. What's the rush?"

He gave her an enigmatic grin. "I'll tell you outside."

Knowing he wouldn't give her what she wanted until they left the building, she let him take her elbow and usher her outside and then stopped on the sidewalk as the glass front doors swung shut. "What did you find?"

"I printed out some reports. They're in your purse."

Her eyes went wide. "I thought this felt heavier

than usual." She started to take the bag off her shoulder but he stopped her.

"Let's get out of here."

"Anything good in the reports?"

"I didn't take the time to look. I figured you and your watchdog would be back shortly."

Falling into step beside him as he hurried toward his truck, Blaise grinned. "From where I stood it looked like she was watching you, not me."

He shook his head, oblivious. It was one of the things she loved about her hunky fiancé, he had no idea how gorgeous he was. Women's heads swiveled all around them as he opened the door and handed her into the truck.

A gooey bubble of happiness warmed in her belly at the knowledge that he was all hers.

Blaise's phone rang as Dolfe circled the truck to climb inside. It was Ty. "Hey! What's up?"

"I was wondering if you'd spoken to Suz today?"

Blaise glanced over as Dolfe slammed the driver's side door and scanned her with an assessing glance. His green gaze narrowed in question.

She shook her head. "I haven't. You didn't expect us to come in today, did you?"

"No. It's just that...well..."

She suddenly understood. "You were supposed to see each other today and you haven't heard from her."

A beat of silence made Blaise smile. He hadn't

known she knew. "Don't worry, Suz didn't tell me. I could tell by the way you two were acting."

"That obvious, huh?"

"To a phenomenal student of human nature, yes."

"And a modest one."

She shrugged, even though he couldn't see it. "What can I say, I know my strengths." And weaknesses. But she wouldn't dwell on those. "I'm sure she just got wrapped up in something and forgot. You know how she is." Suz was Blaise's best friend... aside from Dolfe of course...but she was one of those Type A personalities who could easily lose herself in whatever she was doing, fighting to achieve perfection and momentarily forgetting that the world around her existed.

"Yeah, it's just..."

"What?" Blaise didn't like the tone in Ty's voice. "Talk to me."

"She was going to come back to the bar this morning to get her tips and clean up after the police were here. She called and left me a message around ten and it was garbled. You know how bad the cell phone reception is at the bar."

"Unfortunately, I do."

"Well, it sounded like she said she'd found something. By the time I got the message she wasn't returning my calls."

Blaise frowned. Dolfe turned to her and she held up a finger. "Maybe her phone ran out of juice."

"No. It's fine. I'm looking at it."

A cold dread razored through Blaise's middle. "What do you mean you're looking at it?"

"I'm at the bar. Suz's car is here. The place looks like somebody held an MMA match here and..."

Blaise heard him take a shaky breath. She turned to Dolfe, speaking in an urgent whisper. "The bar. Hurry."

"Her phone was on the floor, her purse was still on the bar and... Blaise, there's blood."

"We're five minutes away. Don't touch anything else," she instructed her friend before hanging up and grabbing hold of the door and the dash as Dolfe whipped the big truck into a U-turn and slammed his foot down on the gas.

T y's older Chevy truck was parked next to Suz's tiny sedan at the outside edge of the parking lot. The lot was empty other than that, with only a few discarded paper cups and other detritus fluttering across its broken asphalt surface.

The front door was unlocked and, when they moved out of the sunshine into the softly lit interior of the bar, Dolfe blinked to adjust his vision.

The first thing he noticed was the overturned

chairs and the general disarray that hadn't been there the night before. Then he spotted Ty, sitting at the bar with his back to them. The owner didn't turn around as they approached. His head was lowered, his gaze locked on whatever he held in his hand.

Blaise touched the man on the shoulder. "Ty?"

When he looked up, his eyes were filled with tears. He shoved Suz's phone across the bar toward Blaise. Dolfe recognized it because of the abundance of bling on the case. "I'm the last person she called." He sniffed, shaking his head. "And I wasn't there when she needed me."

Blaise pulled the man into a hug. "We don't know she's in trouble, Ty. Maybe there's a perfectly innocent explanation for all this."

"If you can find it, I'll be thrilled."

Blaise looked at Dolfe, her brown gaze imploring. "Show me where you found her stuff," he told the bar owner.

Ty motioned toward the stockroom door as he slid off the stool. "Her phone was in there. I found her purse and keys on the bar there..."

Dolfe glanced where Ty pointed. Sure enough, a small, leather bag sat at the end of the bar with a set of keys on top of it.

"She always drops her stuff there when she comes in."

They followed him through the door behind the bar. The walls of the long, narrow room were lined with shelving. Dozens of bottles of booze, wine and beer covered the shelves. At the end of the room, a small, high window let the sun ease through to paint a stripe down the floor. Ty led them to a spot at the end of the stripe, where a case of beer had been tipped off the lower shelf. It still rested there, as if someone had set it down in surprise or dropped it in the act of lifting.

"Her phone was just under the shelf, there." Ty's finger pointed to a spot near the leg of the shelving unit. "I almost didn't see it because it was mostly under the shelf." He scrubbed a hand over his mouth, looking worried. "The sun caught on her bling and it sparked."

Dolfe was only half listening. The concrete was darker in one area on the floor. "This spot here is damp. Do you know what it is?"

Ty shook his head. "No. I noticed it too."

Dolfe touched a sparkling dust peppering the wet area and pulled his finger away. "This is crushed glass." He scraped the dust into an evidence bag and pulled an evidence swab from his pocket, running the tip through the moist area. "I'll send this to Brita for evaluation."

"It's..." Ty swallowed hard. "It's not blood, right?"

"No." Dolfe stood up and slipped the swab into its container. "But you said you found some blood?"

Ty blinked, seeming to snap out of his dark thoughts. "Yeah. Over here." He guided them to the short wall with the window and pointed to the floor. Dolfe crouched down and saw several spots of a brownish red substance on the floor. "This blood is old."

Ty let go of the breath he seemed to be holding. "Thank God." He and Blaise shared a smile. "It's not hers," Blaise said happily.

Dolfe scraped up the blood with his pocket knife and added it to a small bag. "We'll test it to make sure." He stood. "Most likely one of your employees had a minor injury over the last week or so."

"Highly possible. We're always slicing our fingers on cut glass and stuff," Blaise said.

"As happy as I am to learn that isn't Suz's blood, it still doesn't explain where she is."

Dolfe spent a few minutes looking around the area in the bar where it appeared there'd been a scuffle. To his dismay he did find some blood on the floor beneath one of the overturned chairs. It wasn't a lot. Not enough to worry that Suz had been dispatched in the bar, but there were a few drops leading to the back door.

As Blaise kept Ty distracted, Dolfe took a sample of the blood and then followed the droplets into the alley behind the bar. There, he found more evidence of a struggle and a pair of skid marks on the rutted asphalt.

He pulled out his phone and called Brita. She

answered on the second ring, sounding even more tired than she had that morning.

"Hey, it's Dolfe. I think you need to get over to *Tyrese's Bar*. Suz Whatsnoggin has gone missing and there are signs that she might have been abducted."

B laise couldn't believe it. She just couldn't believe it. First Roger White dead and wrapped around a toilet and now Suz was missing? She watched Brita and Dolfe walk the alley, listened to the comforting drone of Dolfe's deep voice as he explained what they'd discovered inside and how he'd come to be in that alley in the first place. It all felt so surreal. She couldn't imagine how Tyrese felt.

Turning to the bar owner standing beside her, Blaise linked her arm through his and squeezed it. "Dolfe will find her. He's really good at this."

Ty nodded but didn't respond. He didn't turn his worried gaze from the cop and the PI.

"Tell me exactly what Suz said to you when she called."

He shook his head. "Not much. Just that she was here and she'd found something weird. She asked when I'd be in."

"Did you ask her what she'd found?" Blaise knew it was a dumb question. If he knew what Suz had found he'd have already told them. But she needed to keep him talking in the hopes he'd give her information he didn't know he had.

Dolfe had taught her that.

"No. It didn't occur to me. Now I wish I had."

She squeezed his arm again. "There's no way you could have known."

"Who would have done this? And why? How would anybody even know what she'd found?"

"Maybe it isn't connected." As soon as Blaise said the words she wanted to take them back,

Ty's eyes widened in alarm. "If it's not, what does that mean? You don't think she's been grabbed by a serial killer or something, do you?"

Blaise would have happily smacked herself upside the head. "No. Of course not. I meant maybe she just walked down the street or something. There's probably a perfectly reasonable explanation for all this."

"Believe me, I'd like to believe that but Suz never goes anywhere without that phone. I even have to pry it out of her hand when we..." He blinked, shrugging with embarrassment. "And she wouldn't have gone anywhere without her purse either."

Blaise knew he was right. She and Suz had been friends for years. Her friend was predictable and responsible. She wouldn't have walked out and left the bar open and her things behind. Not if she had any control. "Who might have been here this time of day? Are there any deliveries scheduled?"

"Delicious Foods."

"Huh?"

"Our food supplier. They deliver on Friday mornings." He frowned thoughtfully. "And the rug company comes around noon to take the dirty rugs and put down clean ones."

Blaise nodded. "That's good. Anybody else?"

"It seems like I might have had a morning meeting scheduled but I can't remember who it was now. My mind's fried from all this..." He swept a hand to encompass the alleyway and the bar. "I would have made the appointment for later though. I don't usually get in here until closer to noon."

"Could Suz have made an appointment?"

"Probably not. I can't remember the last time she did. But if one of our vendors called and asked if they could move up a delivery she'd have agreed since she was here anyway."

Blaise felt hope slide away. "Then it could have been any of them?"

"Any of about a dozen, yeah."

"Not exactly," Brita said as she joined them. "The only person who had a reason to take Suz is the killer."

Ty made a small sound like a wounded animal. "That can't be good."

Shaking her head, Brita glanced toward Dolfe,

who was crouching near a skid mark in the broken pavement. He snapped a picture of the tire mark with his phone. "The killer must have left something behind and come back to get it."

"But how could he have known Suz would be here?" Ty asked.

"He probably didn't. She might have just been in the wrong place at the wrong time. Is it normal for her to be at the bar this time of day?"

"No," Ty said, shaking his head. "She wanted to straighten up after yesterday. I think she was doing it for me..." His voice quavered and he ran a big hand over his jaw, the midnight stubble of his beard crackling against his palm. "I was pretty upset about the mess and all. I'm guessing she planned to surprise me." Tears shimmered in his wide, brown eyes.

Blaise wrapped an arm around his shoulders. "She's going to be all right, Ty."

Dolfe joined them, sticking his hand out, palm up. A tiny gold hoop glistened in the center of his latex glove. The hoop was made up of double gold rings with a tiny diamond fixed at the point where they crossed. "Does this look familiar?"

Blaise's stomach twisted with alarm. "It's hers. It's Suz's."

Ty reached for the earring but Dolfe pulled his hand away. "We need to check it for prints."

Ty's expression tightened, but he nodded. "I can't believe this is happening."

"I'll need a list of everyone who might have stopped by the bar today," Brita told him.

"Sure. I'll go do that now."

Brita nodded. "Good. I'll take her phone in and let our Digital Evidence Techs take a look at her calls and texts. Maybe we'll get lucky and our guy contacted her by phone before he showed up here."

Dolfe dropped the earring into a bag and handed it to Brita, along with the samples he'd collected inside. "Blaise and I will talk to the other businesses around here...see if anybody noticed a van or truck speeding out of the alley this morning."

"Good. Thanks for your help."

Dolfe squeezed her shoulder. "No problem. I'll let you and Percival buy us dinner when this is over."

She laughed. "If he hears you call him by his full name the only thing I'll be buying you is a tombstone."

Dolfe cracked his knuckles. "Brita, he's a lawyer. I think I can take him."

"Keep telling yourself that. Don't forget he's got seven brothers."

"There is that."

Blaise gave Brita a hug and, before she pulled away, whispered into her friend's ear. "Find her, Brit. I'm scared."

Brita patted her back. "I'm on it. See you guys later."

7

The liquor store on the corner next to the bar had just opened its doors when Dolfe and Blaise arrived. The man sweeping the sidewalk in front of the store had rosy cheeks and thick black hair that stuck up as if he'd sucked a lightbulb in his bathtub that morning. He was round with skinny arms and legs and several chins.

The owner looked up when they approached and smiled. "Mornin' folks."

Dolfe nodded. "Morning."

Blaise gave the man a grin and a little finger wave. "Hey, Mr. Butran. How are you?"

"Blaise, honey. I'm just fine now that I've seen your beautiful face."

Blaise's grin widened with pleasure.

Dolfe was sorry to ruin it, but he had a job to do. He showed the man his license. "I'm Dolfe

Honeybun and I was wondering if you could answer a few questions for me."

The store owner stopped sweeping and wrapped both hands around the top of the broomstick. "Sure. Is this about the murder in the bar?" He shook his dark head, folding his pudgy face into a frown. "That was a damn shame. Tyrese must be beside himself."

"He is," Blaise said soberly. "We're helping the police figure out what's going on."

"That's good. I'm sure they can use all the help they can get. Crime in this city seems to be spiraling out of control lately." He eyed Blaise. "But I'm afraid I don't know anything about the murder. I'd already closed the store and gone home when it happened."

"Actually we were wondering if you'd seen a van or truck speed out of the alley between your place and Tyrese's this morning. Probably about an hour and a half ago?"

The man narrowed his hazel eyes in thought. "Like a delivery truck, you mean?"

"It could have been a delivery truck," Dolfe agreed.

"Well, no. But I usually get my weekly beer and wine delivery on Friday mornings. Which is why I wouldn't have seen anything in the alley. I was busy putting stock away."

"Does your delivery company park back there?" Blaise asked. She skimmed Dolfe a quick look and he realized what she was thinking. If Butran's delivery guys were in the alley that morning, they could have been the ones who left the skid marks.

"Nah. They pull up front and unload from there. It's easier to navigate through the store than the hallway in back where the stock room is. Bad planning on that hallway."

"Do you by any chance have a security camera out back?"

Shaking his head, the man gave them an apologetic smile. "Sorry. I just don't use that door enough to worry about it. I have it double dead bolted and I set my alarm at night. Nobody's ever tried to break in." He reached out a fleshy hand and knocked on the arm of a wood bench, grinning. "Do you mind my asking what this is about?"

"Suz was kidnapped from the bar this morning," Blaise said, her eyes shimmering with unshed tears.

"Possibly," Dolfe clarified. He dropped an arm around Blaise and pulled her close, rubbing her arm. She'd suffered a few shocks over the last twenty-four hours and he was proud of the way she was holding up. But sometimes she hid her emotions so well he forgot how affected she was.

The man's eyes went wide. "Sweet little Suz? Oh no. And you think they took her out in a van from the alley?"

"It's the working theory, yes," Dolfe responded.

"Tyrese used to have cameras out there but some kids busted them and I don't think he ever got them fixed." Scrubbing a hand over his chin, he sighed. "I'm starting to worry about the safety of this neighborhood, Mr. Honeybun. First the murder and now this. What's going on?"

"There's a good possibility it's all connected, Mr. Butran."

"You don't think Suz had something to do with the murder?" The man gave Dolfe an admonishing look. "That sweet girl would never do such a thing."

"Nothing like that, Mr. Butran," Blaise soothed. "Just the opposite. She might have seen or found something in the bar this morning that made her a target."

Dolfe almost smiled. Since working with him on a few cases, his party girl had certainly picked up the lingo of an investigation. Dolfe handed the man his card. "If you think of anything..."

"I'll call. You bet I will." He frowned. "There is one thing, about the murder, not about Suz."

"What is it?" Dolfe asked.

"I hear things. Tyrese's customers come in here all the time and they talk among themselves. Sometimes I can't help but hear."

Blaise winked at him. "After a few drinks it's sometimes impossible *not* to overhear them. They get loud and rowdy."

"Exactly." Mr. Butran chuckled. "Lately there's been a lot of displeasure over Ty's new microbrew selection."

"They don't like the microbrews?" Blaise asked on a frown. "I'm surprised. They seem to be really popular. We've doubled the number of customers since he started selling them."

"Well, you see that's just it. The old timers...the ones who've been coming to *Tyrese's* for years, they aren't all that happy about the new clientele. The word 'yuppies' might have been spat out a few times, in none too happy tones."

"Any of these complaints serious enough to represent a motive?" Dolfe asked.

"I doubt it. But I just thought you should know. If you're lookin' for somebody who might have wanted to take out a newcomer at the bar, you might be lookin' for a familiar face."

Dolfe thanked the store owner. Blaise gave the man a hug and promised to stop by for his wine tasting the following weekend.

As they walked toward the store on the other side of *Tyrese's*, Dolfe cut a warning glance in her direction. "You weren't thinking of asking me to come to that wine tasting were you?"

She grabbed his arm, her face morphing into her 'innocent' expression, which really just made her look impish. "What if I was? Why wouldn't you want to go with me?"

He lifted her hand, nibbling on her soft knuckles. "I'd go to the ends of the Earth with you. But I'm not sure my bank account can afford another *wine of the month club* commitment. Besides, there's so much wine in the house now there's barely room for me."

She slapped his arm. "That's such an exaggeration. There's plenty of room for you. All we need to do is build a wine cellar in the basement. Then you can spread out and do all the weird stuff you do again."

"What weird stuff?"

She waggled her brows. "That oldie stuff you call dancing."

He clasped her hand and lifted it, spinning her in a circle and then yanking her in so she was pressed against him from knees to delightfully plump breasts. "You mean like this?"

She laughed, her head dropping back as he began to sway with her on the sidewalk. Traffic sped past, the occasional horns blaring as they danced to the sound of engines, passing conversations and piercing horns.

Dolfe inhaled her delicious scent and felt the world right itself. It didn't matter where they were or what was going on, just having her in his arms was enough to create music in his soul. Music he'd happily dance to no matter where they were.

"Get a room!" somebody shouted good-naturedly.

Blaise pulled out of his arms, a wicked gleam in her brown eyes. "I'll admit, I'm starting to see the appeal of the oldie dancing."

"Right?" Dolfe tugged her hand and they headed for the flower shop next to Tyrese's. "I'll make sure you reap the rewards later."

"Reaping sounds like a perfect way to spend the afternoon."

"You bet your bippy, darlin'."

"That's very presumptuous of you, Mr. Honeybun. If I had a bippy I wouldn't bet it. That would be reckless."

The door to the flower shop jangled happily as they walked in. The sweet scent of flowers overwhelmed Dolfe at the door, creating a tiny niggle of panic in his chest. When it came to selecting flowers for the women in his life, he'd always felt a bit cloddish and unsure. There were just too many choices and he'd learned the hard way that the wrong one could send him spiraling into dangerous territory.

Fortunately, Blaise stepped forward, introducing herself to the woman behind the counter.

"Hello, I'm Blaise and this is Dolfe. We're helping the police investigate a possible kidnapping at Tyrese's."

Dolfe held his license out for the woman behind the counter to inspect. She pursed full lips and sighed, her too-thin face folding into a frown. "What in the world? A murder and now a kidnapping? What's going on over at Ty's place?"

Blaise shook her head. "We think the two things might be related."

"Oh my." The florist dropped onto a stool and let the flowers in her hands fall back into the basket she'd pulled them from. "Poor Tyrese. I just don't understand how these things could be happening in our nice little community."

"We're going to find out, Miss..." Dolfe lifted a brow in question and the woman shook herself, giving them an embarrassed smile. "Sorry. I'm a little discombobulated. I've had two weddings cancel on me this morning. Seems murder is bad for business." She shoved at the discarded flowers, looking sad. Then she blinked and lifted her gaze to his. "My name's Samantha. I own this little bit of heaven." She swung a hand to indicate the shop, which seemed more like Hell than Heaven to Dolfe but he understood he might be in the minority on that. "Were you in the store around ten this morning?" he asked.

"I was. I was working in the front window, freshening my displays."

"Did you happen to see a van speeding out of the alley," Blaise asked.

Samantha blinked. "A van? No. I'm sorry. I tend to get really into my work and lose focus on the world." She shrugged. "Who are you looking for?"

"My friend, Suz," Blaise said sadly. "She works at Tyrese's with me."

"Oh, I know who she is. A really sweet gal. Dangit! This bad stuff needs to stop." Shoving a limp strand of dark hair off her face, Samantha appeared to be ready to cry.

Dolfe sent Blaise a visual SOS and she reached over the counter, clasping one of Samantha's bony hands. "I know, it's very upsetting. But you have to trust the police and my Dolfe. He's just about the smartest man I know and he's going to catch the people doing this."

Sniffling, Samantha ran the back of her hand under her eyes to dry her tears. "I'm sorry. I'm not usually this emotional. It's just...well...I can't afford to lose those weddings."

Blaise sent him a pleading look over the woman's head and his heart started to pound really hard. But he fell into the sexy brown pools of her eyes and couldn't find a way to refuse her unasked question, so he nodded.

Blaise's wide smile almost made up for his bowel-melting fear.

"Well, it just happens that Dolfe and I are getting married soon and we were going to ask if you could do our wedding."

Samantha lifted a tear-drenched gaze to Blaise. "Really?"

"Really," Blaise assured her with a grin.

"Wonderful!" Samantha nearly leapt from her stool. "When do you want to get started?"

Dolfe saw stars and thought he might pass out. "Um..."

"I'm afraid today's not good," his beautiful Blaise said. "We're in the middle of solving this murder and everything."

"Oh," Samantha blinked and sniffed. "You're right. You'll let me know when you're free?"

"I'll call you next week?"

"Perfect!"

Dolfe started backing toward the door. "Well, um, we should…" He pointed hopefully toward the exit.

Blaise looked like she might start laughing any minute. But she said her goodbyes and joined him at the door.

He was pulling it open, relief setting in for having escaped the close call, when the shop owner stopped them.

"Wait!"

His heart started pounding again.

"You might want to check the ATM across the street."

Dolfe and Blaise looked at her, not compre-hending what she was telling them.

"The camera? It might have caught your van leaving the alley. It's kind of pointed that way."

She was right, Dolfe glanced across the street and felt instantly better. Maybe they'd get a break on the case after all. "Samantha, you're a genius."

The woman beamed happily. "I'll see you two

next week. I'm really excited to be working with you."

And just like that he was miserable again.

Dolfe called Brita and within the hour she had video feed of a dented white van screaming out of the alley, a figure wearing a ball cap pulled low over his face driving. The side of the van was unadorned, sporting only the grayish shadow of a previous logo they couldn't quite make out.

Brita put a BOLO on the vehicle and there was nothing left for Dolfe and Blaise to do but head home. Dolfe dropped her at their little white house on a large, treed lot and headed into his office to clean up some emails and do some paperwork.

B laise entered the coolness of the little house and smiled. They'd bought the hundred-year-old, stucco home with the arched doorways and leaded windows a few months back and she'd loved every minute of her time living there. The place was bright and cozy and she felt at home there like nowhere else she'd lived. Part of that feeling, she knew, was because Dolfe was there with her. Part of it was the house itself. It sent out warm vibes, an embracing aura, that Blaise found irresistible.

Entering the newly renovated kitchen that

sported white cabinets, marble countertops and stainless steel appliances, Blaise hung her bag on a hook by the door and spotted the thick sheaf of papers sticking out of the top. The reports Dolfe had copied. She'd forgotten all about them.

She tugged the stack of photocopies out with a grin. Dolfe had been busy while she'd been chatting it up with Ginny the receptionist. She placed the paper on the island and heated water for some tea. A steaming mug in her hand, Blaise dropped onto one of the tall stools at the island and started going through Roger White's laboratory reports.

The house shook under a clap of thunder and Blaise jumped, expelling air as rain started to pound on the house's tin roof. She normally loved the sound of a summer storm, but her nerves were a tad bit shot from recent events and, when she started sorting through the reports, she was surprised to find her hand shaking.

It took her a few minutes to figure out what she was seeing but once she did, she realized Kopper from *Artisan Beers* had been right. Roger had been failing a lot of the microbrews over the last several weeks. Blaise had to wonder if Kopper's accusation of Roger being a purist was true, or if the man had ulterior motives for failing the lab tests.

She examined the findings for *Artisan Beers*. Roger had failed three out of four of their beers. His recommendation for two of them was to dump the batches. Blaise had no idea how much that cost the small brewery, but she was sure it was too much.

And the lost beer was only part of the problem. She assumed fermenting beer was a lengthy process. That time meant additional money lost for a microbrewery. She whistled when she saw how much *Artisan Beers* had spent on testing for the year. "I'm on the wrong end of this business," Blaise murmured. "I should be testing this stuff instead of drinking and serving it."

Next, she went through five other microbrewery reports and was shocked to realize Roger had recommended drastic action on only one beer out of a dozen. It was true, he had found fault with nearly all of them, lending credence to the idea that he was too picky, but his findings hadn't cost the five other breweries their stock.

She realized why Dolfe had copied those particular reports. He'd probably come to the same conclusion Blaise was coming to. Kopper had been right about Roger's intentions where *Artisan* was concerned. But he'd been wrong about Roger's overall tactics. It did seem as if he'd targeted *Artisan* with particularly stringent reporting. But only *Artisan*.

Leaving Blaise to wonder if *Artisan* brewed really bad beer. Or if Roger had it out for them for some reason.

8

*T*he storm was really gearing up, Mama Nature throwing a true tantrum, when the land line phone in the kitchen jangled to life.

Blaise frowned. She didn't think they'd ever gotten a call on the thing. In fact, she'd razzed Dolfe about adding it when they'd moved in. But he'd insisted, saying that a land line might come in handy in case their cell phones failed.

She settled her tea cup onto a small table and climbed out of the comfy window seat overlooking their street. It was her favorite spot to read, watch storms, and generally while away the hours dreaming about her future with Dolfe.

She smiled at herself as she reached for the phone. She was really becoming a romantic sap in her old age. "Hello?"

"Dolfe Honeybun?"

Blaise frowned. If she sounded like a six-foot-five inch, two-hundred-fifty pound man she needed to do something about her hormones and fast. "No. Do I sound like him?"

"Sorry, dude. I meant, can I talk to him?"

Dude? Blaise looked down just to make sure she still had boobs. "He's not here right now. Can I take a message?"

"I need to talk to him *now*. A message will be too late."

She frowned. "Who is this?"

"It's Nathan. He told me to call if I found out anything about the dead guy."

Blaise's antennae sprang to attention. "You mean Roger White?"

"I don't know his name. The guy who was wrapped around the toilet at *Tyrese's*."

"Okay. Did you try calling Dolfe's cell phone?"

"It just goes to voicemail." A fumbling sound made Blaise think he'd hung up. She panicked. "Wait, Nathan?"

"What? You need to help me, man. They're gonna kill *me* next."

Blaise felt her last nerve twang. "First of all, stop calling me *man*. I'm not a man. You're seriously messin' with my self-esteem here."

"Sorry, dude."

She huffed out a breath. "And secondly, I'm

Dolfe's partner. Tell me what you need and I'll help you if I can."

"No offense, man but I need a dude. You're not going to be able to put the smack down on these people like your giant partner could."

"Just tell me who you're afraid of."

"I don't know who they are. But I seen 'em roughin' up one of my clients. Dude was so scared I think he might have pissed his pants."

She fought the urge to roll her eyes. The kid was a serious drama mama. "Okay, that sounds like your client's problem, not yours."

"Well it was, until they shot at me."

Blaise felt her eyes go wide. "Shot at you? Real bullets?"

"It wasn't a water pistol."

Blaise grabbed the notepad off the counter and ripped the grocery list off the top. "Tell me where you are."

"I need to talk to Dolfe."

She bit her lip before she said something everybody would regret. "I'll bring him with."

"You ain't lyin?"

Blaise crossed her fingers. "I'm not lying to you. I'll call Dolfe as soon as I get off the phone with you and we'll come over. Now tell me where you are."

He rattled off an address. "It's an empty old building a few blocks from *OnPoint*. We used to store stuff here but I think it's mostly empty now. Probably why those guys are using it to meet. I followed the guy here because he was actin' weird and after what Dolfe said..." She heard the sound of fabric swishing and figured he must have shrugged.

"Okay, we'll get there as soon as we can."

"Hurry, man. I think they just spotted where I'm hiding. Oh crap..." The line went dead.

She dialed Dolfe's cell and got a busy signal. Something wasn't right. Dolfe always answered his cell. She was torn between driving over to his office and checking on him, and going to help the delivery kid. Finally, she settled for texting Dolfe her destination and heading out the door. She'd call Brita on the way.

Unfortunately Brita wasn't available to take her call. Though she left a message, she...like Nathan... didn't think the message would get to the cop in time to do her any good. She pulled up to the curb in front of a cool old brick building with a broken sign hanging crookedly over the door. The name on the sign was too worn for Blaise to read, but she was pretty sure it didn't say *OnPoint Distributors*. Maybe they'd rented it once upon a time.

She eyed the place but didn't see any movement. There were a couple of pickup trucks parked on the street, one newer and expensive looking and one old and rusted. She had a pretty good idea which truck belonged to Nathan.

Blaise tried calling Dolfe again and got a busy

signal. She shoved her phone into her pocket, grabbed a can of mace from her purse, and forced herself to step out into the rain.

Dolfe dialed the home number again and then Blaise's cell. He got voicemail on both phones. He disconnected, a mix of frustration and fear setting up residence in his chest. It was silly to be worried. He'd taken her home himself. There was probably a perfectly reasonable explanation for why she wasn't answering. For example, the storm had probably knocked out the phone lines again.

Maybe she'd forgotten to charge her cell. He couldn't exactly fault her for that since he'd done the same thing that morning. If Brita hadn't dropped by his office to talk about the White murder he might not have noticed the problem for another hour or so. His cop friend chastised him for not answering and he'd pulled his cell out from under a pile of bills and reports to discover it was dead as a doornail. He'd frowned at the dozen or so calls he'd missed, especially the five from Blaise.

Listening to her message, Dolfe bit back a string of curses. Blaise could easily be walking into a dangerous situation without him. Unfortunately, she'd called almost a half hour earlier so she was probably already at the meeting with Nathan.

He shoved to his feet, grabbing his partially charged cell. He'd have to finish charging it in the car.

Only the comforting realization that Nathan was no killer...Dolfe would stake his own life on it...kept him from calling in Brita and the national guard to head Blaise off.

He'd just have to turn her over his knee later for putting herself in danger.

Now why did that thought make a warm, gooey spot in his belly?

Warm rain pelted him as he ran toward his truck, which he'd parked at the curb in front of his office. He'd transformed an old house in a changing neighborhood into *Honeybun Enterprises Private Investigations* and split his time updating the office building and the little piece of Heaven he and Blaise had bought to start their lives in. It made for a busy, hectic life. One that didn't leave him a lot of spare time to play. But somehow he and Blaise had managed.

He climbed into the truck and turned the key. The engine ground and died. Gritting his teeth, Dolfe tried again, getting the same result. A few minutes later he realized he'd flooded the engine and had to stop. He'd have to give the vehicle a few minutes before he tried again.

Time he couldn't afford to lose.

"Damn!" He slammed his palm on the steering wheel and grabbed his cell, dialing Blaise again. The phone rang several times and then her bright, happy voice answered, asking him to leave a message.

T he door was unlocked. Blaise stuck her head in and looked around. The nearly empty building was too dark to allow her to see much. The uneven outline of something that looked like brewery equipment huddled, partially hidden, under large white tarps, and a few cardboard boxes sat in one corner. Other than that, Blaise didn't see anything.

"Nathan!" she scream-whispered into the stillness.

Nothing.

She stepped through the door, lifting her mace to what would be about eye level for the average sized man. She picked her way carefully through dust and chunks of wood and paper, sidestepping the emaciated form of a dead rat along the way.

Grimacing, Blaise decided to risk snapping on her cell phone light so she didn't step on anything that might fight back. She felt in her jeans pockets and pulled out her phone, clicking on the light.

A muffled thump had her whipping around, her

gaze searching the gloom for the location of the noise. The noise had come from the other side of the building, the muffling suggesting it was separated from the room she was in by a wall. Blaise saw a narrow strip of light along the floor and headed for it.

She found the door handle and gripped it, leaning into the rough, rust-covered surface to listen for more noise. She heard nothing so she risked opening the door. It creaked softly and Blaise stopped, her eyes wide and her heart banging against her ribs.

Silence throbbed across the space, carrying menace with it.

Blaise swallowed hard and eased through the door, letting it snick shut behind her. She looked around, finding herself in a tight hallway next to a water fountain that was tucked into a narrow alcove.

Footsteps echoed off the walls and Blaise backed up, looking frantically around for a place to hide. The nearest door was fifteen feet away in the direction of the footsteps. She judged by the sound of their approach that she didn't have that much time. She jammed herself between the wall and the water fountain and crouched down, tucking her knees beneath the fountain.

Almost too late, she remembered to turn off the light on her phone.

She closed her eyes and prayed whoever it was

wouldn't see her. Her palms were sweaty, but her fingers clutched the can of mace as if her life depended on it.

It probably did.

The footsteps stopped and the doorway she'd been eyeing opened just enough to show a man's tall frame backlit by yellow light. The man didn't make a move to leave, he just stood there for a moment. She squinted, trying to see his face, but he had his head turned away from her. He appeared to be dressed all in black, a black stocking cap pulled down over his hair. The line of his jaw she could see was angular, the skin smooth and jaundiced in the yellow wash of light. The figure was slightly built but seemed strong and agile.

The man stared into the room for a moment, his expression hidden, and then turned away, heading toward Blaise. Panic thrummed along her spine and she tightened her hand on the mace. She made a soft sound of surprise as the small can slipped through her sweaty grip and dropped away. It clanged against the water fountain and then hit the floor, rolling away from her.

A bright light snapped on, blinding her. Quick footsteps slapped against the grimy floor and Blaise realized he was coming after her. She pried herself out of her hiding spot and hurled herself at the door she'd entered through.

The footsteps came on, speeding up. With a

panicked cry, she grasped the door handle and yanked it open just as a hand found her arm, squeezing painfully.

"Don't move," a harsh whisper commanded.

Blaise stilled, trying to see the man's face through the darkness. All she could see was the general shape of his head and face and, judging by the fact that he was looking down on her, the fact that he was a few inches taller than her.

He jerked her arm. "Who are you?"

Blaise shook her head, leaning into the open door with her shoulder. If she could only break his grip and dive through the opening, maybe she could get to the outside door before he came after her.

He yanked her up hard against his body, wrapping an arm around her throat so she couldn't look into his face. "I asked you who you were?"

Her hand was jerked off the handle and the door slammed closed, removing Blaise's escape route. Panic flared as she realized the full extent of the danger.

She was going to die if she didn't think of something fast.

"Um, nobody. I mean. My name is Blanche. I'm thinking about buying this old building so I came to check it out."

She could almost hear the man thinking about her ridiculous statement. Then his arm tightened around her throat and she suddenly couldn't breathe. "I asked you who you are and what you're doing here. Now, this time, you might want to answer honestly. Convince me you're harmless because I've got more to lose in letting you go than in killing you."

She tried to swallow but her throat was constricted. Her lungs screamed as spots danced before her eyes. The panic which had begun as a whisper across her mind had become full-fledged hysterical screaming in her head. Her fingers gripped his arm and clawed it desperately.

He loosened his grip enough to allow her to talk. Blaise coughed violently, swallowing to wet her dry throat. "I'm telling you the truth. My brother's a realtor. He told me this building was about to go on sale. This is prime real estate. I thought I could get ahead of other buyers." She shrugged. "Clearly the building's not for sale. That's cool. Really, no worries. There's another place over on Wilton Boulevard I've been looking at. I'll just go bid on tha..."

Quick movement. The shadows shifted, and pain sheered through her skull, driving darkness into the space behind her eyes.

9

*D*olfe had his gun out and his senses peeled. Seeing Blaise's car outside, parked at the curb behind an old beat-up pickup truck, he'd been peeved afresh that she'd come without him. But as soon as he stepped into the building his internal alarms went off. Every step he took through the too-quiet place made the warnings more strident, until he wasn't sure he could hear if someone screamed his name with the blood rushing through his head.

Like the outside exit, the interior door, which appeared to lead to a set of unused offices, was unlocked. He stepped through, stopping long enough to get his bearings, and then moved into the hall. His foot hit something, sending it pinging down the passageway with a series of metallic clangs.

Dolfe shone his flashlight on the object as it

came to a halt against the filthy rubber strip at the bottom of the wall.

He recognized the tiny canister. It was Blaise's pepper spray. His pulse leapt even higher and he suddenly found it hard to breathe. Dolfe had to take a moment to force air into his chest, striving for calm. He would do her no good if he panicked and made mistakes. She was counting on him to keep his cool and that was what he'd do.

Until she was safe with him again. Then he was gonna go all medieval on somebody's ass for endangering her.

Dolfe slid along the wall, listening and scanning the shadowed space as he walked. He moved quickly, silently, and with the expectation that he might have to react at any moment to an attack.

The gentle scent of Blaise's body lotion teased his senses. A softly botanical scent that never failed to make his body tighten with interest. *Hold that thought*, he told himself. He would get her back safe and then he'd take the time to show her how much she meant to him. He wouldn't even consider any other options.

He couldn't.

If anything happened to Blaise...

His pulse kicked back into overdrive and Dolfe too quickly found himself breathing hard from the adrenaline rush. He really needed to focus on the task at hand.

The first door on the right was slightly ajar. Dolfe peered through the two-inch crack and saw only a battered wooden desk and an ancient coat tree. A tattered, stained cardigan hung from the tree, long ago forgotten by its owner.

Dolfe slowly pushed the door wide and quickly scanned the area. He was just about to move on when he spotted what looked like the bottom edge of a shoe behind the desk.

Panic flared. He stepped into the room, his gun extended as he carefully peered around the age-worn furniture. A body lay in the shadow of the desk, sprawled and motionless, with a pool of dark blood forming a halo around the dark head.

Before he could stop himself, a small cry of horror escaped his lips.

She struggled against her bonds, the ropes around her wrists chafing as she wriggled her hands to loosen them.

She'd been fighting to loosen the stupid things for hours...maybe days...beneath the foul-smelling bag they'd thrown over her head she'd lost track of time.

Nobody had come to check on her for a really long time. Nobody had brought her food or water. Nobody had asked if she had to pee.

Tears burned her eyes at the thought that she was going to die a long, agonizing death of dehydration in that horrible place.

It was cold and damp. Her clothing had grown heavy against her skin with the moisture. Water trickled nearby, tantalizingly close, and the smell of rotting vegetation told her it had probably been running for a long time.

Occasionally something skittered past, causing her to jerk her feet up until they were tucked close to her body. She made herself as small as possible, not knowing where danger would come from and unable to avoid it when it came.

Fear was an icy fist in the center of her chest, making it hard to breathe, even if the rope around her throat wasn't already slowly choking her to death.

She sat as quietly as possible, trying to hear something...anything...that would tell her where she was. But in her panic she couldn't hear anything except the constant trickle of water and the skittering of little rodent feet close by.

Too close.

Beyond tears and exhausted from the emotional and physical mistreatment, she must have dozed off for a while. She was torn awake by the long, low boom of thunder. The air was thick with the smell of rain. A flash of light pierced the fabric of the bag covering her head and another thunderous groan soon followed. The storm was right on top of her. But when rain finally came, an impossible crashing of large, hard drops against the roof high above her head, she realized she was nowhere near the city.

If she were still in Indianapolis she'd hear traffic, horns honking, the occasional bleating siren. The realization brought tears stinging to her eyes again. She was all alone. Abandoned. With nobody to turn to for help.

A sob escaped and she slammed her lips closed over it. She wouldn't give in to despair. She would find a way out of that place. And then she'd find a way back home.

She wouldn't let them beat her.

No matter how low her odds of escape.

"Nathan Lord." Brita looked up from the kid's driver's license and saw the expression on Dolfe's handsome face. He looked like he'd seen a ghost. "You know him?"

"He's a delivery guy for *OnPoint Distributors*." Dolfe swallowed, his throat working hard as if it were parched. "Blaise was meeting him here."

Brita wanted to swear. She scrubbed a hand over her face, feeling like she needed to sit down. She'd failed Blaise when her friend needed her. If only she'd answered her phone when Blaise had called. "I was interviewing Roger White's boss when she called. I should have taken the call."

"You didn't know," Dolfe told her, frowning. "My phone was dead…" His frown deepened as he mentally beat himself up. Brita had seen it before. It was a trait that was inherent in Honeybuns. Her own fiancé was very good at beating himself up when he wasn't sufficiently omnipotent to save the world from itself. "It happens, Dolfe. The reality is that Blaise should never have come here alone. She's a big girl and made her own decision."

Instead of making him feel better, her statement made him mad. He tensed, fixing her with a hostile green gaze. "I won't let you badmouth her, Brita. Not now. Not when she needs our help."

She shrugged, knowing it would only make him more angry. It worked beautifully. He slammed a palm down on top of the scarred wooden desk, leaning closer. "And you call yourself her friend."

Brita held his gaze, unflinching, and waited for him to rise to the occasion. He would. It wouldn't take him long. Honeybun men always did.

Finally he expelled a frustrated breath and started toward the door. "I guess I'm in this alone then."

"Dolfe."

He stopped, one big hand on the door knob, his broad shoulders immobile with anger and fear.

She waited.

Finally he turned back, his gaze tight with fear. "What if she's...?"

"She's not," Brita interrupted. "And you have to be strong. You need to make good decisions."

He drew air into his lungs in a long, deep pull. Then he nodded. "Thanks."

She fought a smile. "For what?"

"For putting starch back into my spine. I know you're not blaming her. But if I even let myself think..."

"Don't go there, Honeybun. Our girl is alive. Right now she's probably making the bad guy wish he'd just walked out the back door when she arrived."

Dolfe gave a bitter laugh, shaking his head. "Truth."

"Detective Muldane?"

She looked up as a uniformed cop came into the room, his gloved hand held out in front of him. Something golden lay in his palm. "We found this in the back. It looks like somebody was being held here."

She looked down at the oversized gold hoop earring. "Dolfe?"

He was suddenly there, reaching for the earring with a cloth handkerchief. He held it up and narrowed his gaze as the light sparked off the jewelry. "It's Suz's. The mate to the one we found at Ty's place."

"Yeah, that's what I thought. Well that definitely connects the murder to Suz and Blaise." Brita nodded to the uni. "Show us where you found the earring. Then I want you to bag it and put it with the other evidence."

The uniform took them to an old boiler room, a narrow, dank space that held the electrical guts of the building. Rusted pipes traversed the low ceiling and dropped into the concrete floor. A length of chain and a padlock rested on the floor around one of the vertical lengths, giving testament to the fact that someone had been held there.

"We found the jewelry tucked in behind the pipe, like someone had jammed it there."

"Good girl, Suz." Dolfe crouched down and ran a finger over a dried brownish red spot near the pipe, frowning. "Dried blood."

"Probably from her restraints. I wouldn't read anything into it." Brita eyed Dolfe as he straightened, no doubt wondering if he was going to come unglued again. He had no intention of losing focus. He was back on track.

"She's leaving us bread crumbs." He started for the door. "Let's see if we can find more of them." Finding the back exit, Dolfe went outside into a weed-strewn parking lot and located a piece of bling near the door. If he wasn't mistaken, it was one of the fake gems from Suz's phone. She must have somehow kept hold of it when she'd struggled with her captor.

Brita took the dark pink gem, frowning. "Suz's?"

He nodded. "I'm pretty sure it came off her phone." He expelled a long breath, fighting the panic that sat just beneath his ribs and clamped icy fingers around his lungs. "I think it's safe to assume that we're no longer trying to save one woman. Whoever took Suz clearly also has Blaise."

"I'm going to find Kopper. So far everything we've learned points to *Artisan Beers* or him. At least that's a good place to start." Dolfe took off running toward his truck as Brita turned to her uniforms and instructed them to get CSU to the sight and to lock everything down until they arrived.

10

*S*he was in some kind of truck. She knew that because the vehicle was really loud and took every bump as if it had no shocks. Blaise was woozy, her head throbbing in time to her heartbeat, and there was something stiff and drying on the side of her face. She suspected it was blood.

She tried to lift her hand to touch the throbbing spot but it wouldn't move. She struggled to remember what had happened. As her mind cleared, she realized someone had hit her alongside the head with something metal. Maybe a gun. Clearly whatever it was had opened a wound on her head. But other than the pounding headache she seemed to be all right.

Her wrists were bound behind her with something rough that had already torn the skin. She struggled against her bindings but was unable to loosen them. All she succeeded in doing was tearing her skin up worse.

She lay across a bench seat, the sun blinking over the blindfold covering her eyes as if they were driving underneath a lot of trees. That, as well as the rancid stench of cow manure told her they were probably somewhere within the miles of open country outside Indianapolis.

Gravel crunched beneath the tires, supporting the country road theory. Occasionally the vehicle's back tires skidded sideways as the driver took a turn too quickly.

Her captor's driving was making her sick to her stomach and she wasn't at all sure she wouldn't be anointing his backseat with regurgitated blueberry waffles.

When the vehicle finally stopped Blaise realized it was her chance to make a move. She had no idea where they were or what the guy had in mind, but she knew she had to get away. Her captor had killed one person already...maybe two...and he surely wouldn't hesitate to kill her too. The front door slammed and Blaise tightened her stomach, pulling herself upright with monumental effort.

Hard hands grabbed her arm, tugging her off the seat.

She leaned back, fighting the extraction, and when her captor leaned in to grab her with both hands she kicked out hard, connecting with a soft belly.

He let go of her and she stumbled forward, praying she found the ground without falling on her head. The man sucked in a wheezy breath, telling Blaise she'd either hit him in the gut or the family vault. Either spot should slow him down.

She fell into the door and shoved her feet downward, clipping her ankle painfully on the edge of the door. As soon as her feet hit the ground she threw herself forward, pushing the door back with one hip as she started to run. She couldn't see anything past her blindfold but she didn't intend to let that stop her. As soon as she got some distance she'd find a way to scrape the blindfold off her eyes.

The ground was uneven and she almost went down. A hand scrabbled for her leg and she realized her captor was either bending over or on the ground.

Good! She must have hit him hard.

Blaise fought the instinct to slow down and pick her way forward. Her only chance was to put some distance between him and her. Unfortunately she didn't get far. She stepped down and the ground disappeared from under her.

She screamed as she fell and kept on falling, hitting water and going under before she could drag in a panicked breath.

Flailing frantically with her feet, she felt rough

walls in all directions. Finally, when she thought she would surely drown, she found a protrusion on one wall and got one foot onto it, surging upward until her face barely cleared the water. She dragged in a quick breath before she fell off the small ledge and went under again.

She sank all the way to the bottom of what she realized had to be a well. The bottom was slimy and when she jammed her feet against it and pushed, her shoes slipped and she cracked her head on the wall. She tried again, earning herself enough traction to shove upward and break through the surface of the water. The light beyond her blindfold faded and she realized someone or something was blocking it. It was probably her kidnapper, checking to see if she was dead.

Taking a quick breath, Blaise let herself sink silently below the water's surface. If she was lucky he'd think she was dead and leave. She held her breath until her lungs felt like they'd burst and then forced herself to rise slowly to the surface.

Blaise listened carefully and heard nothing. After a few minutes she figured he was gone. Kicking to stay above water, she leaned into the wall and carefully scraped the blindfold against the rough surface. It was wet and sticking to her face. By the time she finally got it to slide down her face, she thought she must have scraped half the skin from her cheek and temple.

Lying back in the strong smelling water, she let herself float on the surface and examine the well as best she could. The sun only reached a few feet into the well and the rest was shrouded in darkness. The opening looked to be about twenty feet above her head. The brick walls, with the exception of the ledge she'd found with her feet when she fell in, was relatively smooth. There were a few similar protrusions from the old brick, but they were spaced too far apart for an easy climb to the top.

The water was cold and black, stinking of minerals. She guessed nobody had used the well for a long time. Which meant nobody was going to wander up with a bucket and rescue her. She was on her own and she needed a plan. But as long as her captor didn't come back she had a little time to figure out what to do next.

First on the list was getting her hands free. Then she needed to figure out how to get out of the well. Next she needed to find her way back home. But to do that she was going to have to locate civilization. If her hunch was right she was out in the middle of nowhere.

The enormity of her task was depressing and she was suddenly sure she would fail.

"No, dammit!" Blaise shook her head, blinking away tears. "I need to do this." The thought that Dolfe was probably frantic, looking for her, gave her the motivation she needed to fight.

She took a deep breath and went back under the water. Finding the ledge she'd stepped on before, she swung around and awkwardly began rubbing the ropes binding her wrists against the sharp edge of the soggy brick.

After a minute she had to come up for air. But she forced herself to drop back under again. Severing the thick rope was going to take a while. But she didn't have a choice. She couldn't climb out of the well with her hands bound. She'd have to unbind them.

***

The receptionist they'd spoken to the last time he and Blaise had visited *Artisan Beers* was seated behind her desk, a glass and chrome monster that seemed way over-sized for the laptop and phone that were the only items on its surface.

Dolfe pushed through the front doors and headed for Kopper's office.

"Excuse me!" The woman's chair squealed as she shoved it back, all but jumping to her feet.

Dolfe didn't slow or respond. He headed down the hallway and shoved the door to the manager's office open.

It was empty.

The receptionist rolled in behind him, storm

clouds in her eyes. "Can I help you?" Dolfe was pretty sure, judging by her tone, that she wasn't really sincere about wanting to help.

"I need to talk to your boss."

She crossed oversized hands at her waist and cocked her head. "What's your business with him?"

"Police business. Where is he?"

The receptionist lost some of her starch. "Is everything okay? Has Mr. Kopper been hurt?"

"Not yet. We'll see how he is after I talk to him. Where is he?"

Her worried expression transformed into one of anger. "You can't come in here threatening people, Mr...?"

He strode closer, towering over the woman. She shrank back in fear. Dolfe felt bad about that, but she was currently standing between him and finding Blaise. "I haven't begun threatening yet. I believe he had something to do with the abduction of my fiancée. Now you have about three seconds to tell me where he is or you'll be charged as an accessory to her abduction. And if she's harmed in any way, I'll make sure you go to prison along with your boss."

She blinked rapidly a few times and then started to quiver. Placing a supporting hand on the back of a nearby chair, she shook her head. "I haven't seen him since I came in this morning."

"Where did he go?"

"I don't know. I promise I'm not lying. He got a call from Alex Byerson..."

"Who's that?"

She looked shocked that he didn't know. "The owner of *Byerson Beers*."

"Was it unusual for the two men to talk?"

"A little, yes. They've known each other for years in a professional capacity of course. But I don't think Mr. Byerson has ever called here befo..."

"Where is *Byerson Beers*?" Dolfe interrupted.

"Oh...it's just a couple of miles up the road. Only about five minutes..."

Dolfe shoved a business card at her. "Call me if you hear from your boss." He hurried out of the building and climbed into his truck, calling Brita as he swung around and headed toward *Byerson Beers*.

She answered on the second ring. "Dolfe, I just got a call from Alex Byerson..."

"He called Kopper this morning and now Kopper's MIA."

"I know..." She hesitated a moment. "How did you know that?"

"I just spoke to the receptionist at *Artisan*."

"Byerson seemed concerned about Kopper. Said he was acting very strangely."

"I'm heading to *Byerson's* now. I'll talk to him," Dolfe promised.

"Good. Let me know what you find out. In the

meantime, I wanted to let you know the ME gave us a finding of poisoning for Roger White's death."

"From the e-cigarette?"

"I'm sure that's what the killer wanted us to believe. But that would imply his death was an accident and with everything else that's going on I doubt it."

"Agreed," Dolfe told her.

"Also, that glass you scraped up had traces of nicotine and other flavorings on it. That matches the ingredients in the liquid you swabbed up too."

"e-Liquid? What would a vial of e-Liquid be doing in Ty's storage room?"

"Maybe the killer dropped it. If White was killed, nicotine could be the poison of choice for our murderer."

Icy dread swept through Dolfe. The killer had Blaise. It wouldn't take him long or be too difficult for him to dose her too.

"I'm heading over to Kopper's house." Brita told him. "If he's running, that's the first place he'll go."

The light ahead turned yellow but, rather than stopping, Dolfe pressed the gas, speeding through the intersection on a mostly red light. "I'll call you after I talk to Byerson."

The parking lot at *Byerson Beers* was emptying out when Dolfe pulled in and parked. He realized with a start that it was almost six o'clock. The day had fled. It also meant darkness would come in a few hours and Blaise would be officially missing. There was something about heading into evening with a missing loved one that made it seem terrifyingly real. The darkness made their disappearance more terrifying. Once the sun went down, only bad things happened to people who'd been abducted.

Dolfe shook off the dire thoughts and cut the engine. The car next to him pulled out and left, leaving only Dolfe's truck and a low-slung silver sports car in the lot. He hoped the sports car belonged to Byerson. He didn't relish having to hunt down both he and Kopper to get answers.

Byerson's Beers couldn't be more different from *Artisan* if it tried. Where *Artisan* seemed to be striving to resemble an old-style brewery, with retro touches and a classic feel to it, *Byerson's* felt more modern. Situated in a newer, blond brick building with very little in the way of adornment, Alex Byerson's namesake felt like a business rather than a sentiment.

To Dolfe's surprise, the man himself was waiting inside the lobby doors, leaning against a tall counter with a guard seated behind it. He hurried forward when he saw Dolfe, manicured hand outstretched.

Dolfe quickly took the man's measure. Combining prior knowledge of the family from the social pages of the *Indianapolis Star* and his first impressions, Dolfe decided the thirty-something owner probably viewed the business as something he indulged in between trips to the French Riviera or the Swiss alps. He wore perfectly pleated charcoal gray slacks, a black turtleneck and a charcoal gray jacket. The clothes fit him too well to be off the rack and the ring he fiddled with on his right hand appeared to have some kind of family crest on it. When the man spoke, the impression of entitled wealth was solidified. His voice was smooth, cultured and almost British in its pronunciation.

"Mr. Honeybun. I'm so pleased you're here." He pumped Dolfe's hand and nodded toward the elevator. "If you'd rather we can speak in my office."

"That won't be necessary. I understand you spoke to David Kopper this morning."

Byerson frowned. "I did. A very strange conversation."

"He's missing and I need to find him."

Byerson leaned nonchalantly against the high desk, his carefully combed dark hair glistening under the overhead light. "You believe he had something to do with Roger White's death, don't you?"

"What do you know about that, Mr. Byerson?"

"The microbrewery world is small, Mr. Honeybun. News travels fast. I heard Roger was poisoned."

"Do you have any reason to suspect Kopper might be behind his death?" Dolfe asked.

Byerson shrugged. "White was known for his exacting standards. Let's just say that *Artisan* didn't always rise to those standards."

"He failed them a lot in his testing?"

"Often enough to sting."

"It's a long way between irritation at getting bad test results and killing a man."

"True enough. I'd guess it would take a certain temperament to commit murder."

"And you believe Kopper had that temperament?"

Byerson straightened away from the guard desk. "You must believe so since you're looking for him."

Dolfe didn't miss the careful way Byerson implied Kopper's guilt without coming right out and stating his suspicion. "I'm actually looking for him on another matter."

Byerson looked intrigued. "Oh? What matter?"

"Can you tell me why you called Mr. Kopper this morning?"

"I...yes...I was calling to tell him that I'd promoted one of my employees to New Accounts."

"Dierdre Masterson."

His gaze widening with surprise, Byerson nodded. "Yes. How did you...?"

"Small world," Dolfe reminded with a smile.

"Yes. Of course. I knew David had been trying to lure Dierdre to *Artisan* and I wanted to tell him she'd accepted my promotion."

Dolfe lifted a skeptical brow. "You believed that would stop him from trying to hire her?"

"Not really," Byerson chuckled. "But it was worth a shot."

Dolfe nodded. "How did Mr. Kopper seem to you when you spoke?"

"Agitated. He blew in here with a chip on his shoulder and he was wild-eyed...almost unhinged."

"He came here?"

"Yes. I thought the news would sit better if it was given face to face."

Dolfe doubted that was the reason. Byerson probably hoped to intimidate the other man into backing off. "He was agitated before you spoke to him about Miss Masterson?"

"He was. He parked that big pickup in front of the door and stomped into the building, screaming my name." Byerson frowned, appearing upset with the encounter.

"What time was this?"

Byerson glanced toward his guard. "Hollis, can you check the log?"

The guard nodded, his dark brown gaze skimming over Dolfe with a tinge of hostility before looking down at the book in front of him. He ran a blunt-tipped finger along the handwritten list of names and stopped, poking a name on the page. "Around noon, Mr. Byerson."

Close enough to the time Blaise was taken. "Was there anyone else in Kopper's truck?"

Byerson looked at Hollis. The big man shook his

head. "I'm sure there wasn't. I met him outside and told him he couldn't park there. He shoved past me and went inside. I was near enough to the truck that if there were someone else sitting inside I'd have noticed."

Dolfe nodded. "Why was he so angry, Mr. Byerson?"

Byerson shoved his hands into the pockets of his slacks and looked down. He stared at his expensive black loafers for a long moment and then sighed. "I'm afraid that's my fault. He'd found out I'd taken Roger White out to dinner a few days ago and he accused me of setting *Artisan* up."

"Did you? Set him up?"

"I don't have to resort to those tactics, Mr. Honeybun. My beer is better than *Artisan's* swill."

"Then why did you take Mr. White to dinner?"

"I take all my vendors and partners out on a regular basis. They like the special attention and it ends with them feeling kindly toward me and my operation." He shrugged. "It's just good business."

Dolfe's phone rang and he looked at the display, answering it quickly. "Brita."

"Kopper's gone. It looks like he's running. But I think you'd better come over here, Dolfe. There's something I need you to see."

"Text me the address." He disconnected and shook Byerson's hand again. "Thanks for your time, sir."

"Anytime. I hope I helped."

Dolfe turned away and hurried out of the building without responding. All he could think about was what Brita might have found at Kopper's house and what it had to do with Blaise.

He was almost afraid to know.

———

11

*B*y the time Blaise managed to break through the ropes, her hands and arms were numb from the cold and the sky above was a gorgeous array of sunset colors. She really wished she could enjoy the colors, but she had no idea how she was going to climb out of the well. There were only a few jutting chunks of brick in the entire well and they were too wide-spread to use as a ladder to the top.

Blaise floated on the surface of the inky water and eyed the walls. She had an idea and prayed the well was narrow enough across for it to work. Using the small ledge as a starting point, Blaise hoisted herself up and perched her butt on it, praying it would hold. It wasn't nearly deep enough to sit on comfortably, but hopefully she wouldn't need to stay there long. Leaning against the wall at her back,

Blaise stretched her legs out and fell off the ledge, plunging into the icy water and dropping to the bottom.

She shoved off the slimy bottom, slipped again and caught herself against the wall before she cracked her head. But as she broke the surface of the water, she threw back her head and screamed in frustration.

Then she indulged herself with a good cry.

The darkening of the sky beyond the opening was all the impetus Blaise needed to stop feeling sorry for herself. If she didn't get out of that well before it got dark she'd be working in pitch black conditions. She didn't fool herself into thinking a fat, silver moon was going to cast light down the well to guide her way.

Her best shot was to get out of there while she could still see.

She shoved herself back onto the ledge and extended her legs again, pointing her toes until they reached the other side. Pressing against the wall, Blaise realized her toes were never going to hold all the way up. She arched her back and managed to flatten her feet against the wall. Happy she was wearing sneakers instead of her usual heels, Blaise took a deep breath and shoved against the wall with her shoulder blades, walking her feet up a few inches. Then she pressed her sneakers against the wall and, using her hands to help, shimmied upward a few inches.

Her back and calves started screaming after only going only a couple of yards.

By the time she'd gone half a dozen feet she was in tears. But by the time she was an arm's length from the top the pain had become almost white noise in the larger problem waiting for her above.

As she'd neared the top of the well, she'd become increasingly aware of a crackling noise and the sharp scent of burning wood. The air above the well was dense with a gray haze she realized was smoke. But it wasn't until the terrified shrieking started that Blaise realized what she was up against.

Somebody was trapped in the fire she could smell and hear.

Beneath the strident threads of pure terror in the chilling screams was a familiar note. Blaise recognized the voice. And it made her clumsy with renewed fear. Her feet slipped and, before she could stop herself she'd slid downward almost eighteen inches.

Blaise screamed in frustration and dug in again, determined to get out of that well to save Suz.

Dolfe pulled up behind Brita's unmarked car and killed the engine. He took a minute to gaze around, wondering if Kopper's neighbors might know where he'd gone. Brita had already put a couple of uniforms to work interviewing the ones who were home. The cops were talking with small groups of neighbors as he climbed out of his truck. An array of curious gazes followed him when he turned toward Kopper's home.

Someone called his name and he turned to see Brita walking toward him down the street. He was a little surprised to find her out there instead of in the house.

"This way," she told him, motioning him toward the curb a couple of blocks up. The street was crowded with cars. Most of the neighbors seemed to use the curb for parking their extra vehicles. Dolfe didn't see the van until he'd walked a half block up the street. It was snugged in between a minivan and a large SUV.

His pulse picked up at the sight of the boxy white vehicle. "Is that our van?"

Brita pointed to the open back doors and he stuck his head inside, finding the single gold bangle lying half hidden among a pile of dirty tarps. An evidence marker sat beside the bracelet. "Does that look familiar?"

He frowned. "I don't think it belongs to Blaise," he told the cop.

"No," a deep voice said from around the front of the van. Dolfe peered around the open doors and saw Tyrese strolling over, his dark face creased with worry and fatigue. "It's Suz's. I gave it to her for her last birthday."

Dolfe let his eyes go wide. "Kopper's our kidnapper?"

"It sure looks that way. We'll know more after the lab processes the truck," Brita told him.

Dolfe shook his head. "He's apparently not very smart...parking this on his own street."

"Yeah, it seems a little too pat, doesn't it?" Brita frowned too.

Tyrese stopped beside Dolfe, his lean form taut with anger. "What are you waiting for, arrest this asshat and make him tell you where Suz is."

Dolfe knew how he felt. "I'm sure Brita's doing all she can to find him."

She nodded. "We put a BOLO out on his vehicle. A late model Ford pickup truck. But so far it hasn't been located."

"What about the house?" Dolfe asked. "Nothing there to tell us where he might have gone?"

"He has a cabin up north, near the Michigan border. I've contacted authorities there and asked them to do a drive by."

"Seems unlikely he'd take Suz that far away and then come back and grab Blaise," Dolfe mused.

"I agree. But we need to make sure."

Tyrese leaned against a tree and scrubbed a frustrated hand over his face. "I can't believe this. Suz has been gone too long. She's probably terrified. We need to do something, Dolfe. I'm going crazy just sittin' around waitin'."

Dolfe nodded. "I know how you feel, Ty."

12

*B*laise wrenched herself upward, over the lip of the well and collapsed on the cool grass for only a couple of beats, just long enough to catch her breath. The screaming had stopped a few minutes earlier and that really concerned Blaise. She pushed to her feet, her muscles cramping with weariness, and started loping toward the burning building in the distance.

She crossed a heavily weeded gravel road and a wide expanse of scrub grass to a line of boarded up buildings that looked like they hadn't been inhabited in decades.

Flames licked from between the boards in one building, the aging wood already charred as it gave way to the hungry fire. It looked as if it had once been some kind of restaurant. The metal roof was bent and rusted, smoke pouring toward the sky. The front had been mostly windows, with a broken door in the center, but the glass that remained was jagged and glittered on the cracked and weedy sidewalk beneath them. Smoke poured from every orifice, coating the buildings on either side of the restaurant and clogging the air Blaise was gulping in big swigs.

She started to cough as she pulled tiny slivers of ash into her lungs. Yanking her shirt off over her head, Blaise tied it over her nose and mouth and kept moving.

Flames danced above the tin roof, reaching fiery fingers toward the roofs on either side. She quickly realized she wouldn't be able to get inside through the front, which was fully engulfed, so she ducked into an alley and headed blindly toward the back.

The smoke was thick in the debris-strewn alley and her lungs labored beneath it. She stumbled over refuse, nearly going to her knees before catching herself on the wall of the burning building. Even the building's exterior wall was hot and she worried that whomever was inside wouldn't be able to survive for long.

Her eyes stung so badly she couldn't keep them open. Tears flowing, Blaise mopped continually at her streaming eyes and prayed she'd reach the end of the alley soon.

Finally, she emerged into air that was only mildly less smoky. But at least the smoke was thinner and she could just make out a door hanging open at the back of the building. Smoke poured from the door but there were no visible flames. If she was really lucky the blaze was centered at the front of the building and she'd be able to get in, grab whoever was in there and get out before fire consumed the rest of the building.

Taking a deep breath through her shirt, she dove inside and squinted through the hazy darkness, panicking as she realized she couldn't see a dang thing.

She moved carefully forward, taking care not to touch anything metal. The heat in the small building pulsed against her skin, making her woozy.

Her foot hit something heavy and she went down, the body she'd stumbled over taking the brunt of her fall. Unfortunately she cracked an elbow against the grungy floor and pain radiated up her arm into her shoulder. "Crap!" She held her elbow and sucked air as she scrambled to her knees. The form lying across the doorway was male, bulky, and very dead.

Blaise tried to grab him under the arms and pull him out of the building but he was too heavy.

She straightened, trying to form a plan when something smacked the bottom of her sneakers. She jumped, swung around and saw a slim form crumpled in the corner. Blaise let out a scream and hurried over to the woman with the cloth bag over her head. She yanked off the bag and realized it was Suz.

Blaise hugged her tightly. "I can't believe I found you."

Her friend's eyes were wide and tears flooded her eyes. "How in the world...?"

"No time for explanations." Blaise examined Suz's situation and realized she was cuffed to the footrest bar at the bottom of the counter. "We need to hurry..." Blaise succumbed to a bout of violent coughing as she eyed the rope that was looped around Suz's throat and trailed down to her bound wrists. "Let's get you out of here," she choked out.

"I've been trying to get loose but..."

Blaise slammed her foot down on the bar. It tilted away from the wood it was bolted into but held. Three more kicks got it loose and she quickly slipped Suz's binding over the end and helped her stand.

They hurried out of the building, slowing only to step over the dead man.

They headed for a tiny pavilion area in the center of what Blaise was beginning to realize was a small, abandoned town, collapsing onto a chipped wooden bench.

Suz swallowed hard, grimacing, and coughed. "My throat is on fire."

Tugging her sooty shirt off her face, Blaise grimaced. "I bet. We'll try to find you some water in a minute." Blaise grinned. "I know where there's a well but I don't think you want to drink the water in it."

Suz coughed again, the sound husky. "I'll drink anything right now. Where is it?"

"I'm serious about you not wanting to drink it. I'm pretty sure I peed myself when I fell down there."

Suz blinked. "Oh. Oh my god, you're drenched. You fell into a well?"

Blaise wrapped an arm around her friend's shoulders. "I'm okay. I'll tell you about it later. Right now we need to figure out how to get word to Dolfe."

Suz's gaze slid back to the burning building. Flames were finally licking out the back window. "That guy had a phone. I heard him talking on it."

"You're sure someone else wasn't here?"

"I'm not sure. I didn't hear any other voices. But I had that damn bag over my head."

"You're lucky you did. That, and the fact that you were sitting on the floor probably saved your life."

Nodding, Suz asked. "How'd you find me?"

Blaise stood up. "I'll tell you in a minute. I'm going back in for that phone."

Suz grabbed her arm. "You can't! Look at those flames. You'll get burned."

Blaise tugged gently away. "I'll be fine. I'm wet and I'm going to be fast."

Suz pushed to her feet. "If you're not out in three minutes I'm coming in after you."

Blaise took off running, her heart pounding violently as flames snapped through the broken glass of the window a few feet from the door. She'd have to move fast. The idea of searching a dead body made her stomach do painful flips but if it would help her get back to Dolfe she could do it.

She stopped in front of the door and tugged the shirt back up over her face and then, taking a deep breath, plunged through again.

Flames licked at her as soon as she was inside. She smelled burning hair and slapped at her head, spinning around in a panic and singeing her arm as another tendril of the raging stuff found her. Folding herself into as tiny a target as possible, Blaise clamped down on the urge to run shrieking from the building. She fisted her hands and breathed shallowly, fighting for calm.

Then she realized time was spinning past and dropped to her knees, feeling her way along the floor until she felt the doughy form of the dead guy. Wincing with revulsion, she felt along his body until she found his belt. She ran her hands over the fabric of his jeans and yelped as she touched the one spot she never wanted to touch on a dead guy.

"Sorry, totally a mistake," she murmured. She didn't want to be accused of taking advantage of a dead guy's unbreathing state to feel him up. Her fingers found a pocket and she felt along the outside, not feeling a hard rectangular shape. She found the other pocket and it was empty too.

Her heart pounded painfully in her chest. The fire licked closer, encroaching in all directions as she fumbled with the body. It roared threateningly and spit foul, smoky air that seemed to eat through the thin fabric of her shirt and squeeze her lungs. Blaise gave herself thirty seconds before she'd need to vacate, phone or no phone.

She grasped his belt and yanked, rolling him partially over. It took another, adrenaline fueled tug to bring him over onto his back. She shrieked when she saw his face. It was shiny with black blood. The front of his shirt was covered in the stuff too, including the pocket where she saw the tell-tale rectangle of his phone.

Something cracked, long and loud, and the front ceiling crashed down. Blaise screamed as boards slammed to the floor all around her. Something hit her shoulder and pain sheered through her. Suz was suddenly there, screaming Blaise's name. Blaise realized she was lying on her back and the room was spinning behind a hazy cloud. Suz grabbed Blaise's hand and screamed into her face.

"Come on! We need to get out."

Blaise's mind was as foggy as the air spinning around them. A deep, pulsating ache throbbed down her entire right side and she could barely hear her friend screaming her name through the ringing in her ears.

But somehow Suz managed to wrench her to her feet and, together, they stumbled back out of the building.

They were barely ten feet away when the rest of the roof collapsed inward and the dying building let out a long, husky groan.

They collapsed into the grass.

"Are you okay?" Suz asked her, coughing.

"I think my shoulder's broken."

"Let me see." Along with an assorted array of other jobs, Suz had done a brief stint as an Emergency Med Tech. "I'll bet that hurts like the dickens."

Blaise sucked air under another wave of agony. "You have no idea."

Suz patted Blaise's arm. "Actually, I do..." She stood up and moved around Blaise, placing both hands on her shoulder.

Blaise yelped, trying to wrench away. "Don't touch it that hurt..."

Agony, bright and fulsome, roared through Blaise as Suz grabbed the arm and yanked it hard. Blaise screamed, scrambling away from her friend. "Are you crazy?"

Suz grinned. "Feel better?"

Blaise frowned. The shoulder pain was gone except for a dull ache. "You're a sorcerer."

Suz laughed, wiggling her fingers. "Magic hands. It was dislocated. You're welcome."

"If you ever do that again I'll kill you slowly with nail clippers."

Suz's grin widened. "Toenail clippers?"

"Of course. I wouldn't want you to suffer needlessly."

They shared a laugh, the humor easing some of the tension from their adventure.

Finally, Blaise dropped back on the grass, gasping for breath. "I was so close to that phone."

Suz didn't respond. Blaise was almost afraid to look at her friend. She didn't want to see the disappointment on her sooty face.

Slowly, she turned her head and felt her eyes go wide.

"Yes, I have an emergency. My friend and I were abducted and we don't exactly know where we are."

Blaise jerked upright. "You got the phone!"

Suz winked. "Yes, I'll hold." She pulled the phone away from her ear. "They're tracking it right now."

"I don't know whether to smack you or hug you," Blaise said, only half mad.

Suz lifted a hand, wiggling her fingers. "Magic hands, remember?"

13

*D*olfe wasn't able to wait at home a minute longer. He'd gone to the precinct and was waiting for Brita in the bullpen. She was coordinating the search for Kopper and had instructed Dolfe to wait at her desk. Instead of sitting, he'd been pacing the space for over an hour.

He heard a door whisk open and closed and looked up, finding Brita hurrying toward him. "Anything on Kopper?"

"Nothing yet. But something else has happened."

He fought disappointment and reached for his coffee. "What?"

"Somebody tried to kill Deirdre Masterson in the hospital."

Dolfe's stomach lurched. "Is she all right?"

"Yeah. Shaken up of course. She was sleeping and woke up to a pillow over her face. Fortunately my uniform guard interrupted the guy before he could do any real damage. Unfortunately he got away."

"How'd the attacker get past the guard in the first place?"

"She was told I was on the phone." Brita sighed. "It looks like somebody's tying up loose ends."

Dolfe didn't need her to explain exactly what that meant for Blaise and Suz.

They were quickly running out of time.

"I'm going back to Kopper's. I can't sit here anymore."

His phone rang. Dolfe frowned at the number on the display. He didn't recognize it but realized it could belong to a witness who was coming forward with more information so he hit the *Answer* button. "Honeybun."

"Dolfe!"

His heart lurched in his chest and his world trembled. "Blaise, honey. Oh my God! I've been so worried."

"I know, babe. I'm okay. And I found Suz!"

He felt the tension that had been turning him to iron over the last several hours ease away. Suddenly his knees couldn't support him anymore and he dropped into the nearest chair. "Thank god. Where are you, Beautiful?"

"I'm heading home. The local police picked us

up and put us in an Uber. I'll be at the house in about twenty minutes."

Dolfe was on his feet and moving toward the door. "I'll meet you there, honey. I can't wait to see you."

"Me too. I love you."

Tears burned his eyes. "I love you too, Beautiful."

He disconnected and looked at Brita. "I'm going home. Blaise just called. She and Suz are safe."

Brita closed her eyes, her shoulders easing. "Thank goodness." Nodding, she headed back to her desk. "Let me get my stuff. I'll follow you over." She dug her gun and holster out of her desk drawer and grabbed her purse. "Oh, I meant to tell you, that van parked at Kopper's house…" She headed in his direction. "It doesn't belong to him."

Dolfe frowned. "Oh? Who's is it then?"

"A guy named Alvin Sparks. You remember him?"

The name was vaguely familiar. Dolfe held the door for Brita and then followed her out into the lobby. She greeted the officer at the front desk and they left the building. The night was warm and quiet, the street outside the police station nearly empty at nine o'clock. Most people were home, watching their favorite television shows and snuggling. He felt a wave of wistfulness on the heels of that thought. Right at that moment he'd like nothing more than to snuggle up with Blaise.

They left the long, two-story, red brick building that housed the Southwest District of the IMPD behind and headed for the street. Brita stopped beside his car. "I'm in the back lot."

Dolfe nodded. "I hope you don't mind if I go ahead. I'm anxious to see her...make sure she's okay."

Brita smiled. "Of course. I'll be right behind you."

Nodding, he strode into the street and grabbed the driver's side door handle. That was when a memory surfaced of a burly guy with dark hair and shaggy eyebrows, annoying the hell of him with his sexist comments about Blaise. His head came up. "Brita!"

She turned his way, the street light perfectly capturing the slender eyebrow lifting in silent question.

"I remembered who Alvin Sparks is. I interviewed him at *Tyrese's* the other night."

Brita nodded and started toward him. "He was there the night of the murder. I couldn't remember talking to him myself but I had his interview in my folder. What did you think of him?"

"The guy was kind of a jerk. He was pissed off because Ty was selling the fancy local beers and it was bringing in new clientele."

"Not much of a motive but if the guy's an angry sort I guess it would be enough." She looked up at

Dolfe. "The van is enough to at least tie him to Suz's kidnapping and we're looking for Blaise's DNA too."

"Hopefully when they get here they can tell us who kidnapped them."

"Yeah," Brita agreed. But as she turned back toward the gated police lot in the back, Dolfe didn't think she looked hopeful.

"Can you describe the guy who took you?" Brita asked Suz again. They'd been at it for over an hour and Blaise could feel Brita and Dolfe's frustration. Suz couldn't tell them much more than they already knew.

Suz shook her head, her bright blue gaze dim with weariness. "I'm sorry. He was wearing something over his face and when I woke up I had a bag over my head."

"Can't we finish this tomorrow? Suz has been through enough for today." Tyrese tightened his arm around her shoulders. The two of them were pressed so close together on the couch there was still room for Dolfe and Blaise on the other end.

Dolfe sat on the arm of the big piece of furniture, one hand touching Blaise protectively. "Ty, we need to do this if we're going to find out who took them."

The big man sighed. "I know. But Suz is exhausted. She's been through hell."

"And I smell like a campfire," she complained, wrinkling her delicate nose. "I'd like to go home and shower."

"Just bear with me for a few more minutes, Suz," Brita said. "Can you do that?"

Suze nodded, shaking her head as Ty started to argue. "It's okay, Ty. I want to help."

"Good," Brita smiled. "Now what were you doing when the guy grabbed you?"

"I went into the storage room to get some refills..."

"What refills? What part of the room were you standing in?"

"By the bottled beer. I was going to chill a couple of cases."

"Go on." Dolfe urged.

Suz nodded. "I was pulling a case of beer off the shelf when something behind me moved. I started to turn and that's when he hit me."

"Did he knock you out?" Dolfe asked.

"No. Dazed me a bit. He tried to pull something over my head and we struggled. I heard a small sound, like something hitting the floor, and stepped on what felt like a tiny bottle. The glass crushed under our feet. The guy made a sound, like I'd made him angry, and swung at me again. I tasted blood that time. I think I bit my tongue." She shook her head. "It's all a bit fuzzy now."

"You're doing great," Brita assured her. "Then what happened?"

"I managed to shove him away and ran into the bar. We struggled there and I fell. He jumped on me and held me down." Tears slipped from her pretty blue eyes.

Ty glared at Dolfe.

He ignored the other man. "You're doing really well, Suz."

She sniffled, running the back of her hand under her nose. "He must have had his arm around my throat. I remember having trouble breathing and then I think I passed out. When I woke up I was tied up in that horrible place and all I could see through the bag over my head was the shifting light outside."

"We'll get to that in a minute," Brita told Suz. "Thanks for going over everything again."

Suz nodded, leaning into Ty as he kissed her forehead.

Brita looked at Blaise and she knew what was coming. "You want to know how I got grabbed?"

Brita nodded. "Please. Go slowly and tell us everything you remember."

"I got the call from Nathan..." Blaise swallowed hard, remembering the dead delivery guy behind the desk. "He wanted Dolfe to meet him at that warehouse."

"But you went without me."

Her gaze snapped to his, looking for the condemnation she expected there. But all she saw was love. And relief. "I'm sorry. I know I shouldn't have gone alone. But I couldn't reach you or Brita."

He lifted her hand and kissed the back. "No recriminations. I'm just grateful to have you back."

Tears burned her eyes and she nodded, sniffling. "I had a bad feeling when I went into that building. It was too quiet. I was in the hallway, thinking about calling out for Nathan, when the door to the office opened and someone was standing there."

"Did you get a good look at him?"

"No. He was dressed all in black and it was mostly dark. I saw the side of his face, a jawline and cheek, and that was about it."

"Impressions? Age, height, weight?" Brita urged.

She frowned thoughtfully. "Thirties maybe. He carried himself like a younger man. Five ten maybe. Not heavyset, lean in fact..."

"Doesn't sound like Alvin Sparks."

"Who?"

Brita pointed to the phone she'd taken from Suz. It was in an evidence bag. "We ran the phone you took off the guy in the burning building. It belonged to a man named Sparks."

"He was in the bar the night Roger was killed," Dolfe told her.

Blaise's eyes went wide. "He's our killer?"

"We don't know," Brita said. "All we know right now is that his van was used to kidnap Suz."

"And possibly you," Dolfe added.

Blaise shook her head. "No. I was in the backseat of a pickup truck."

"I thought you couldn't see where you were?" Dolfe asked.

"I couldn't. I was blindfolded and my hands were tied with rope behind my back. But I know what the backseat of a pickup truck feels like."

Ty and Suz were snickering before Blaise realized how her words sounded. "I mean..." Her cheeks heated and Dolfe waggled his brows. "Thank goodness experiences from our early dates have finally come in handy."

She smacked him. "As I was saying..." She recounted the rest to them. How she'd been hit, woken up in the backseat of that truck, and fought off her kidnapper only to find herself plunging into the well. She downplayed the well thing because Dolfe turned green when she talked about falling into it with her hands tied and the blindfold on and she didn't want to upset him any more than necessary.

"Then she came and rescued me," Suz said, grinning.

"I heard someone screaming and was afraid it was Suz," Blaise admitted.

"What was Sparks doing when you got to the burning building?" Brita asked.

"He wasn't doing anything." Blaise frowned at

the memory of falling over his corpse and thinking it was Suz.

"He was already dead," Suz agreed. "He was in there with me, telling me that I'd better have friends or family with money because I was only worth keeping alive if somebody agreed to pay a ransom for me. I was trying not to cry. I didn't want to give him the satisfaction. Then he suddenly got really quiet. He told me to keep my mouth shut and walked out the door, slamming it behind him.

"There was a shout and, a minute later, the door slammed again. I heard what sounded like somebody getting hit and then a heavy thump against the floor. I know now it was probably him hitting the ground. A few minutes after that I smelled smoke. That was when I started screaming for help."

"When you stopped screaming I thought for sure you were..." Blaise shuddered.

Suz reached over and grasped her hand. "I decided screaming wasn't helping me get out of there so I concentrated on getting free instead."

Dolfe and Brita were too quiet. Blaise glanced at them and saw the matching worried looks on their faces. "What's wrong?"

Dolfe squeezed her hand. "Nothing. You did good, Beautiful." He leaned down and gave her a gentle kiss that lingered with promise.

Brita stood to go. "That's enough for tonight. I

might want to ask you more questions in the morning."

Suz and Blaise nodded.

"What about Sparks?" Tyrese asked.

They all looked at him and he frowned. "That guy came into my bar almost every night. I can't believe he was part of this. I think he had a sister who lives here in Indy. Is somebody going to tell her? What about his body?" Tyrese's brown eyes were weary and sad. He shook his head. "I just can't believe he kidnapped Suz."

"The fire's out and the local police are keeping watch on the scene until I get there. I wanted to talk to Suz and Blaise while everything was fresh in their minds. I'll focus on Sparks now. We need to figure out what happened to him."

Blaise's weary brain finally put two and two together and she realized why Dolfe and Brita had been frowning. The killer was still out there. And the body count was piling up. As long as he was loose, nobody in the vicinity of the murder at *Tyrese's* was safe.

And that included not just her and Suz but Tyrese too.

14

*D*olfe saw Ty and Suz to the door after they said their goodbyes. Suddenly overcome with weariness, Blaise leaned back on the comfy couch and closed her eyes. She listened to the rush of wind against the windows that probably presaged a pretty good Summer storm and was glad she was safe, at home, with Dolfe.

Then she thought of Roger and Deirdre and realized how lucky she'd been. Despite facing a horrendous danger in the well and inside the fiery building, she'd come out okay. With only some minor bumps and bruises to show for it.

Some, including Alvin Sparks, hadn't been so lucky.

The couch dipped and she smiled as delicious heat spread along her side and strong arms pulled her close. Dolfe kissed his way along her throat, his big hands rubbing her belly in warm, soothing circles.

Blaise sighed. "That feels nice."

He nuzzled her ear and she giggled, scrunching up her shoulder. "Ticklish!"

Dolfe mumbled something that sounded naughty before nibbling on her ear. "Let's get you to bed. You look exhausted."

She shook her head. "I don't want to sleep." What she meant was that she was afraid of the dreams she'd have. She'd been making light of her adventure in the abandoned town, but it had put its stamp on her and Blaise feared she'd suffer under its touch for a long time to come.

"We don't need to sleep."

Blaise's eyes popped open. "Now you're speaking my language."

He kissed the end of her nose. "If your language includes me rubbing your feet until you relax and then holding you in my arms until morning then, yes, we are."

She reached out and touched the sexy fullness of his bottom lip. He looked down at her with such love in his long-lashed green eyes Blaise caught her breath at the sight. She ran her fingers through the thick blond curls that barely touched his neck and pulled him closer. "I'm more interested in having something else rubbed."

"I don't know. You look pretty beat."

Blaise stilled, her gaze sliding over his square, bristly chin and along the muscled neck to the place where his denim shirt was open in an intriguing vee. She licked her lips, running a finger down his throat and into that enticing vee. "I'm not tired anymore."

Dolfe captured her hand as she started to unbutton the shirt, impatient suddenly to divest him of it. "Blaise, we need to talk about what happened to you."

She dipped her head to kiss the sexy place at the base of his throat. "Mmm."

He inhaled sharply as her fingers slipped beneath his shirt and skimmed over his rock-hard abs. "Blaise..."

She moved quickly, twisting out of his grip and spinning to straddle his lap. He gasped as she positioned herself over the hard heat at the junction of his thighs. "I'm trying to be sensitive, woman."

She chuckled softly. "I know. And it's adorable. But right now I want metrosexual you to skedaddle. I'm interested in alpha male you."

He looked shocked. "Take that back."

She grinned, her fingers finding his hard nipples and pinching them just enough. "Take what back?"

"That metrosexual thing. I'm not some girly man."

She twisted her hips and he sucked air, his eyes rolling closed. "Would you say you're a man's man?"

Dolfe's hands found her hips and he tried to

hold her still. "I refuse to be classified. I am what I am."

She nibbled his lip, his delicious breath bathing her face as she licked the soft crease where they met. "Yes you are. And I want what you am...right now."

She squealed as she was suddenly airborne, the steel bands of his arms wrapped around her thighs and buttocks as he stood. "Woman, I'm taking you to bed."

Blaise swooned playfully. "I thought you'd never ask."

He headed for the bedroom. "I'm not asking, I'm demanding."

She frowned. "Now, let's not take it too far. I don't want you to go all Neanderthal on me."

"Ugga bugga," he growled.

Fortunately, Blaise was laughing too hard at that point to argue. And once he'd bounced her unceremoniously onto the bed and covered her with his long, hard body, she had much better things to do than talk.

"Still no sign of Kopper?"

Blaise nibbled on her toast and watched the way Dolfe's shoulders flexed under his shirt as he talked on his cell and made coffee.

"Okay. What do you want us to do?" He listened

for a moment and then nodded. "You got it. I'll talk to you later."

"What did Brita say?" Blaise asked.

"She wants us to stop by the hospital and talk to Deirdre. The guy who attacked her got away and the hospital's cameras didn't catch him. It's like the guy's a ghost."

"Maybe he is?"

Dolfe stared at her over his coffee cup. "Explain."

Shrugging, Blaise wadded her napkin up and threw it onto her plate, carrying it to the sink. "Maybe we should look at a military connection."

He frowned as he considered her idea. "He certainly knows how to sneak around. But so does a good thief."

She dropped her rinsed plate into the dishwasher and closed the door. "You're right. I guess we need to look at both."

"Are you ready to go?"

"Five minutes. I need to grab my shoes and purse."

They parked in the hospital lot and Dolfe climbed out, scanning the area as he walked around to get Blaise's door. He helped her out and wrapped an arm around her waist. "You look very pretty today, future wife."

She cocked a hip, nudging him with it. "You like the colorful hues of all my bruises and scrapes?"

"I like anything on you, Beautiful."

She let the warm glow of pleasure slide over her as they entered the hospital. Dolfe gave his name to the receptionist and told her his business there.

"You're the liaison from the police?" the middle-aged black woman asked.

"Yes. We're here to speak to Deirdre Masterson."

"She's been moved to the top floor. It's a more secure area." The woman gave him a key card. "That will get you onto the floor and someone there will point you in the right direction."

They thanked the receptionist and entered the elevator. Access to the fifth floor required that Dolfe use the key card and, when the door opened on the floor a hospital guard was standing there. "I'll need to see some ID," the man told them.

They produced their identification and the guard checked a list on a clipboard for their names. "You're good to go. Just check in at the nurses' station for the location of your patient."

A few minutes later they were following a young nurse down the hallway toward Dierdre's room.

Deirdre was sleeping when they entered. She was so still and pale Blaise thought for a moment she was dead. "Dolfe?"

He walked over and put his hand in front of Deirdre's face. "She's breathing."

Blaise pulled air into her lungs and nodded, chiding herself for being so jumpy.

A man in an IMPD police uniform entered the room and hurried toward them, one hand on his gun. "Please tell me who you are and what you're doing here."

Dolfe pulled out his license. "I'm Dolfe Honeybun and this is my associate, Blaise."

The gray-haired cop's face softened as he recognized the name. "Detective Muldane sent you."

"Yes."

"Officer Brenton. It's nice to meet you both. I've heard a lot about you." The cop smiled, his eyes twinkling.

"I'll bet." Dolfe nodded toward the woman on the bed. "Is she all right?"

"Sir?"

"She's very still," Blaise said.

"Ah. Yes. She's heavily sedated. As you can imagine she had some trouble relaxing after waking up to find a pillow over her face."

Blaise skimmed the cop a hostile glance, thinking he was making light of Deirdre's close call. But his distinguished face was fixed in a frown. Apparently he was just a shoot from the hip kind of guy. "Did you see the attacker?"

Brenton flinched. "Me? No. I wasn't here when it happened. My partner, Joanna Reese was. She only left for a moment to take a call at the nurse's station.

Thankfully, Miss Masterson knocked a pitcher off the table in the struggle and Joanne heard it. She hurried back and was bowled over at the door by a guy wearing black pants, a black turtleneck and a ball cap pulled down low on his face."

"Can she describe him?" Dolfe asked.

"She gave Detective Muldane everything she had but it wasn't much. It happened fast. She was on her heels or butt for most of it, and the guy kept his face averted."

Dolfe nodded. "Brita said he hid his face from the security cameras too."

"The guy's smart and athletic. Joanna's young but she's a big girl and strong. It takes a lot to put her on the ground. This guy seemed to know exactly where to hit her to send her sprawling."

"Or he just got lucky," Blaise offered.

Brenton shrugged.

"How much of a description did she give Brita?"

Brenton glanced at Dolfe. "Height, weight, facial features from the nose down."

"Was he just under six feet tall, around one seventy-five, clean-shaven?" Blaise asked, picturing her attacker in her mind.

"Yeah, sounds about right. Do you have the guy in custody?"

"Not yet," Dolfe said. "But he's been busy."

"Blaise?" Deirdre's voice was husky and she cleared her throat after she spoke.

"Hey, D." Blaise hurried over and grabbed a water glass, filling it from the pitcher on the table next to the bed. Deirdre accepted the glass gratefully and swallowed a few sips before handing it back. "I feel like somebody stuffed my head with cotton."

Blaise smiled. "It's probably the drugs. Are you feeling okay other than that?"

Her friend reached up and touched the bandage on the side of her head. "Got a headache from this and my neck's sore. I bruised a couple of ribs in the crash..." She shrugged, dropping back to the pillow with a soft sigh.

"In other words you feel like dog doo?"

Deirdre chuckled and then grabbed her head with one hand and wrapped an arm protectively around her middle. "Don't make me laugh. It hurts."

"Sorry. We just wanted to see how you are."

"We?"

Blaise turned and motioned to Dolfe. He joined her beside the bed and Blaise linked her arm through his. Leaning down, Dolfe grasped Deirdre's hand, giving it a squeeze. "You've had quite a time, haven't you?"

Tears filled her eyes and she pulled her hand from his to brush them away. "Sorry. I've been an emotional wreck." She shook her head, her gaze sliding to the cop in the doorway. "I can't believe somebody tried to kill me...twice."

"Do you have any idea why?" Dolfe asked.

"Everybody keeps asking me that!" She groaned, grabbing her head and ribs again. "I've been going over and over everything but I have no idea. It has to be tied to Roger somehow but I have no clue how. I never did see him that night. I just talked to him on the phone that once and agreed to meet him at the bar." She stared across the room, her gaze filled with fear. "Believe me, if I knew what this was about I'd tell you so you could catch the guy."

"Do you think it was the same guy who ran you off the road?" Dolfe asked gently.

She blinked as if she hadn't thought about it. "Same guy? Well, yeah, I just assumed it was." She tried to sit up and went pale, lowering herself again. "You don't think I have more than one person after me, do you?" Panic threaded her voice.

Blaise shook her head. "No. Not at all. Just the opposite. We were wondering if you could tell us anything about the man who attacked you both times."

"I didn't see the driver. Not really. The window was tinted and he only lowered it a few inches to shoot through." She shuddered at the memory. "I couldn't see anything when I was attacked here. There was a pillow over my face."

"Beyond sight," Dolfe urged. "Anything else you remember about him? Smell, touch, jewelry you felt on his hands or wrists maybe?"

She started shaking her head and then seemed

to let his question sink in. "I've been focusing only on the fact that I couldn't see him."

Blaise sat down on the side of the bed. "Will you try something for me, D?"

Her friend looked worried. "What did you have in mind?"

"Nothing scary. I just want you to close your eyes and remember. Try to get past the fear and see if you remember any details you didn't know you had."

Deirdre shuddered again. "I don't think I can do that."

"Sure you can. You want to help us find this guy, right?"

Deirdre hesitated and then nodded.

"The Deirdre I remember from high school was tough as nails. You didn't take any guff from anybody."

Frowning, Deirdre said, "I was much younger then."

Blaise gave her an encouraging smile. "You can do this."

"What exactly do you want me to do?"

"Just lie back and close your eyes."

Deirdre slid Dolfe a worried glance and then did as Blaise asked.

"That's good. Now think back to yesterday. Remember what it felt like to wake up to the attack."

Deirdre stiffened, her eyes moving beneath her lids.

"Stay calm. You're safe now. Nobody can hurt you. Just try to float above the situation and examine it without the emotion. What was the first thing you became aware of?"

"A sound."

"What kind of sound?"

"Shoes scuffing against the floor near my bed."

"You were awake when it happened?" Dolfe asked gently.

"Almost. I was just coming out of a deep sleep."

"Go on," Blaise encouraged. "What happened next?"

"My pillow was pulled out from under my head and I couldn't react in time..."

Blaise patted her friend's hand. "You're doing great. When the pillow was moved, did you open your eyes right away?"

Deirdre opened her mouth to respond and hesitated. "I..."

"No emotion," Blaise reminded. "You're just thinking back."

"I did open them. I saw a flash of white as the pillow came down onto my face."

"And before the white..." Blaise asked her friend. "Was there anything?"

"Blackness." Deirdre shuddered.

"What was black?" Dolfe asked.

"I don't..." Deirdre shook her head and her hands fisted in the sheets.

"No emotion. You're safe here," Blaise reminded softly. "Where was the black?"

"Over the pillow. It was just a slash, like I blinked or something."

"Okay, that's really good, D. Now tell me what you smelled. Was there anything...distinctive?"

"I'm not sure, I..." She nodded. "Yes. There was something. It was just a whiff before the pillow covered me but..."

"What was it, D?"

Her friend's eyes snapped open and she turned to Blaise. "Smoke. My attacker smelled like smoke."

15

*D*olfe flung an arm around Blaise's shoulders and kissed her on the nose. "Where'd you learn that fancy mind trick you used on Deirdre?"

She shrugged. "You always make fun of me for watching crime shows on TV."

He laughed, hugging her close.

He unlocked the truck as they approached and helped her inside. "Where to next?" she asked him eagerly.

"I'm taking you home. After yesterday, you need to get some rest."

"Not a chance! I want to help find the guy who almost killed Suz and me."

Dolfe shook his head and closed the door. He tried to come up with a good argument for making her do what he wanted her to do but he knew there weren't enough words in the world.

When Blaise made up her mind...

Sighing in defeat, Dolfe opened the driver's side door and found himself on the receiving end of her strong opinions on the matter. Basically those opinions consisted of the idea that he was being overprotective and that she intended to help him solve the case whether he wanted her to or not. And didn't he want her to stay with him so they could have each other's backs? After all, look what happened to her when she went off on her own...

Dolfe held up a hand, slicing her off midsentence. "Stop talking."

She frowned and crossed her arms over her chest. "I'm not backing down on this."

He started the truck and headed toward the street.

"Dolfe?"

"I give in. You can come with me. I don't have the strength for any more of your arguments."

She grinned. "I knew you'd see it my way."

He threw her a warning frown. "Don't push it, woman."

"Okay. I get it. You're letting me have my way but you're not happy about it."

"I'm glad we understand each other."

"But I really think..."

"Blaise, I swear I'll turn this truck around and take you home."

"I'll just leave again."

"I still have those fuzzy handcuffs." As he uttered the threat something tightened low in his belly and he realized his mistake.

Rather than being cowed, Blaise waggled slender black brows at him. "Now you're singing my favorite song."

He shook his head. "Incorrigible."

"Where are we going?"

Dolfe turned right and headed toward the highway. "To Roger White's place. Brita's people searched it the day after he was killed but she's asked me to take another look."

Blaise sat back in her seat, biting the lush fullness of her bottom lip. Dolfe was tempted to ask her if she was reconsidering going with him. But he knew his fiancée too well to hope that would work. She'd made up her mind and there was very little in the wide world more rigid than Blaise's determination.

In fact, if there was anything less unbreakable he'd yet to find it.

Roger White had lived in a two story apartment complex made of rusty white brick. His apartment was one of four on the first level and it was in the back, facing a concrete and grass open area with a small in-ground pool at its center.

Dolfe inserted the key Brita had given him and they entered the stale smelling apartment. Blaise's nose wrinkled under the stench. "What is that? It smells like the floor behind the bar at the end of a busy Saturday night."

Dolfe nodded. "Spilled beer." He headed toward the kitchen, which was severed from the rest of the apartment by a short counter. He walked around the counter and stopped, grimacing. "Somebody had a tantrum."

Blaise joined him in the kitchen. "That's a growler from Ty's." She frowned. "I remember when he ordered them. He was so proud of his new logo."

The logo in question was currently broken in half, part of the mess of fractured ceramic and stinky beer residue spread across the tile floor. Dolfe dialed Brita. "Hey, Brit, when your people searched White's place was there a broken beer growler on the kitchen floor?"

He listened for a moment, frowning, and then nodded. "Okay, will do." Disconnecting, he turned to

Blaise. "This wasn't here after he was murdered. Somebody's been in here."

"Why on earth would they dump one of Ty's growlers on the floor?"

"Good question." He took pictures of the mess with his phone. "CSU's coming back to test the beer and look for prints but I doubt they'll find anything. Whoever's behind all this is too smart to leave prints behind."

She nodded her agreement. "I guess we should avoid the kitchen until they've done their thing then."

"Yep. Let's search the rest of the house. I'll take the bathroom."

"What exactly are we looking for?"

"If White found something on *Artisan Beers* that Kopper didn't want made public, he'd have wanted to keep it close."

"A report of some kind?"

"Most likely, yes."

Blaise gave him a jaunty salute and disappeared into the apartment's only bedroom. Dolfe headed into the hall bath. He snapped on a pair of latex gloves and lifted the back of the toilet, finding it empty. Then he pulled out all the drawers of the vanity and dumped the contents into the sink, turning each drawer over to make sure there was nothing underneath.

Fifteen minutes later he'd gone through everything, including lifting out the register covers to make sure White hadn't stuffed something into the ducts. He moved into the main living area. The room darkened as a thick bank of charcoal gray clouds passed overhead. Dolfe found a switch for the overhead light and flipped it on. He started with the antique wooden desk on the outside wall, going through everything and checking the undersides of each drawer. When he came up empty he climbed underneath, looking for a hidden niche.

Blaise came back into the room. "I didn't find anything. The police made quite a mess in there. The mattress has been slashed and everything."

Dolfe slid back out and climbed to his feet. "It's doubtful that was the police. I'm guessing our killer searched the whole apartment. Unfortunately, if it was here, he's probably already found what we're looking for."

The cloud outside moved on and golden light bathed the dusty wood floor again.

Dolfe tugged the desk away from the wall and examined the back, finding nothing. "Did you check inside the ducts in the bedroom?" he asked Blaise.

No response. He glanced up, finding her staring out the window, frowning. "Blaise?"

She blinked, pointing toward the window. "What's that?"

The sun slipped away as another bank of clouds

skimmed past. Dolfe peered through the window. "Looks like another storm coming."

Blaise shook her head, turning on her flashlight and focusing it over the woven shade covering the top third of the window. "That."

His gaze slid to where her light was focused and he saw the telltale rectangular shape near the top. "I'll be..." Dolfe went over and felt along the shade, feeling nothing. Whatever was there, it wasn't heavy enough to create an impression. He pulled the shade away from the window and looked at the back. The window covering was lined with thin white fabric to improve privacy. There was nothing on the lining. He separated the fabric from the woven shade and a folded sheet of paper slid out, floating toward the floor. Dolfe bent to pick it up.

"Hello?"

At the sound of the high-pitched, quivery voice, Dolfe quickly slid the paper into his pocket. He and Blaise turned toward the door in time to see an elderly woman holding a small black and white dog with enormous ears in her arms. The dog barked shrilly when it saw them and wriggled in an attempt to get down.

The woman's faded blue gaze was wide with alarm. "Can I help you?"

Dolfe gave her a smile meant to reassure. He held out his laminated license. "I'm Dolfe Honeybun and this is my partner, Blaise. The police engaged us to help them on Roger White's case."

The woman's eyes went even wider. "You think poor Roger was murdered?"

"It's looking that way," he informed her gently. "Are you a neighbor?"

"Yes. I live in the front apartment on this side. "My name's Agnes Clink."

The little dog barked again, its fringe of a tail sweeping the air behind the woman's arm. She settled it onto the floor with a soft groan, clutching her back as she straightened. "This is Ivy. When Roger didn't come home I brought her to my place."

The little dog bounced toward Blaise and kissed her toes through the flip-flops she was wearing, its tail wagging happily. "She belonged to Roger?" Blaise crouched down and petted the little mutt, earning herself another kiss on the tips of her fingers. She laughed softly, clearly entranced.

"He loved her like a child." Agnes Clink sighed. "It's just so sad."

"Do you know anyone who might have wanted to hurt Roger," Dolfe asked.

"Oh, no. Everyone loved him. He was kind to the children and never complained about the barking dog next door." She shook her head, sending the wattle beneath her outsized chin to waggling. "We never had any trouble from him. And he was always first in line to help when someone needed it." Her gaze slid to little Ivy, who had climbed into Blaise's lap and gone belly up for tummy scratches. "That's why I took little Ivy here. Roger would have been devastated if she'd been taken by animal services." Her eyes went shiny. "But I'm afraid, if he isn't coming back..."

Blaise stilled and Dolfe knew what was coming.

"What will happen to her?" she asked Agnes Clink.

"I'm afraid she'll have to go to the dog pound. I can't afford another mouth, no matter how small, and she needs someone who has the energy to play with her. She's quite a handful, that one." Though Agnes smiled fondly at the little dog, her mind had apparently been made up. "The young couple across the way have agreed to take her for me after work tonight."

Blaise's head whipped around and Dolfe knew what he'd see when he looked at her. So he didn't look. "Can't one of the neighbors keep her?"

"No. I've asked all of them."

"Dolfe?"

He reached down and squeezed her shoulder and promptly changed the subject. "Mrs. Clink, have you seen anybody hanging around this apartment who didn't belong here?"

The elderly neighbor nodded enthusiastically. "You two. Well, I thought you didn't belong. Now I know different." She gave him a no-nonsense look. "I take security very serious, Mr. Honeybun. Such a strange name, by the way. I'm the only one in the building who's home all day so they count on me to keep an eye on things."

Dolfe nodded. "That's very kind of you, ma'am."

"It's the least I can do. The young folks here are very good to me."

"Was there nobody else? Maybe yesterday or the day before?"

Agnes frowned thoughtfully. "There was a truck parked out there yesterday. I'd never seen it before so I asked the neighbors about it when they got home. But it was gone by then."

"Can you describe the truck, ma'am?"

"It was big. Silver I think. Or white. Looked new." She glanced at Ivy and smiled. "She seems to like you, dear."

Dolfe barely kept from sighing. The ride home was going to be fraught with...something he was too tired to deal with.

Blaise straightened up and he finally glanced her way. He saw exactly what he'd expected to see in her pretty brown eyes.

She slid her determined gaze from him to Agnes Clink. "We'll take her..."

"To the pound for you, Mrs. Clink," Dolfe finished hurriedly.

Blaise's lips compressed but she didn't argue.

"Oh would you? That would be so kind. The

sooner this little doll gets put into the system the sooner someone who will love her can find her."

Blaise cradled the little mutt like a baby. Dolfe wasn't fooled. Her grip on the noisy little beast was probably unbreakable. "Don't you worry, Mrs. Clink. Dolfe and I will take good care of her."

"On the way to the pound," he tried.

He determinedly avoided Blaise's gaze as he ushered her and Mrs. Clink out of the apartment and locked the door, giving the key to the elderly neighbor. "Do you think you could give this to the police when they come? They should be here shortly."

"Of course. Thanks again for helping me with Ivy. Would you like to come and get her things?"

"No. That's all right. I'll go to the pet store this afternoon," Blaise responded firmly.

Dolfe wanted to groan. He was toast. And despite his intention of fighting it with everything he had, he knew he would lose.

It looked like he and Blaise had just adopted a dog.

16

"Maybe Brita will take her. She already has five. What's one more?" Dolfe said out of sheer desperation.

Blaise didn't bother answering him. She had her face buried in Ivy's fur and was making cooing type baby noises at the dog.

In response, Ivy gave Blaise a kiss on the nose and then turned a liquid brown gaze on Dolfe as if to say, "This is over chump."

"Yeah, I know. You win," Dolfe muttered.

"I won what?" Blaise asked.

When he glanced back her way she was holding the dog high on her chest so the little mutt could look out the window at the passing scenery. He just barely kept from rolling his eyes. "I hope you intend to pay that much attention to me later," he said with a grin.

Blaise's face was lit up with happiness. In that moment Dolfe knew he wouldn't take the dog away from her for anything in the world. "Don't worry, Honeybun. I'll scratch behind your ears when we get home."

"And under my chin?"

"You drive a hard bargain, handsome."

He pulled into the broken asphalt lot behind *Tyrese's Bar* and stopped. Blaise wrenched the door open before he could even climb out. "Woa..."

She stepped out of the truck, a manically smiling and wagging Ivy clutched in her arms.

"Maybe you should leave the dog in the truck."

"It's okay. Ty won't mind. I need to get her some water." Blaise touched noses with the little beast. "You're very thirsty aren't you, Miss Ivy?"

"Well obviously. It's been a whole ten minutes since she drank the last of my water...from *my* water bottle."

Blaise threw him a look and headed for the back door of the bar. Dolfe placed a hand in the small of her back and made faces at Ivy as she blinked at him over Blaise's shoulder.

The self-assured little beast bounced in her adoring new owner's arms and barked happily, wagging her scruffy tail.

Dolfe laughed at the dog's antics. "She is kind of cute, isn't she?"

That comment earned him a kiss on the cheek from Blaise. Dolfe turned his head and captured her soft lips. Before he pulled away, something soft and wet slipped over his chin. He looked down into Ivy's diminutive face. "Did you just lick me?"

"She likes you," Blaise said, grinning. "My Miss Ivy has very good taste."

Ivy cocked her head, one big ear sticking straight up like an antenna and the other drooping forward as if too tired to stand.

The door opened and Dolfe and Blaise turned to find Alex Byerson leaving the building. He glanced at them, holding the door open, and then seemed to give a start as he recognized Dolfe. "Mr. Honeybun?" He offered Dolfe his hand. "We meet again."

Dolfe shook his hand. "How are you, Mr. Byerson?"

A low rumble emerged from Blaise's direction and Dolfe turned in surprise as Ivy tried to leap out of Blaise's arms to snap at the brewery owner.

Byerson snatched his hand back and laughed. "Dogs hate me. I don't know what it is. Maybe they smell my cats."

"You have cats?" Blaise asked in disbelief.

Dolfe wrapped an arm around her shoulders. "Sorry about that. My manners seem to be on hiatus today. Alex Byerson, this is my fiancée Blaise. Honey, Alex owns..."

"*Byerson Beers*." She offered Alex her hand, pulling Ivy around to her other side at the same time. "I've seen write-ups about you in the paper."

He nodded. "We were the first microbrewery in the area. Did you know that?"

"I do now," she told him, grinning. "It's a pleasure to meet you."

"Me too," he told her. He looked at Dolfe. "Any progress finding Roger White's killer?"

"The police have a BOLO out on David Kopper."

"You think he's your guy?" Byerson frowned. "I just can't believe it. This is going to destroy *Artisan* for a long time to come."

"I'll bet you're really torn up about that," Dolfe said with a smile to soften the accusation.

Byerson frowned. "I am. As I said before, this is a small community and we generally try to help each other out. In fact, that's why I'm here."

"Oh?" Dolfe asked.

Byerson glanced toward the bar. "I just thought, with everything going on, *Artisan Beers* might not be able to fill their orders for a while. I offered to cover them at no cost to *Tyrese's* until *Artisan* gets back online," he explained.

"That's very kind of you," Dolfe said carefully. Clearly the man was either ruthlessly opportunistic or a genuinely kind person. With *Artisan* out of the way, Byerson had a prime opportunity to grab a chunk of their business. Dolfe's cynical nature made him tend to believe Byerson was being an aggressive business man, but he was trying harder to take Blaise's example and see the best in people.

"Well, I should get going. I need to get with *OnPoint* to set up several new deliveries." Byerson smiled at Blaise. "I'm glad you got back safely, Miss Runa."

Ivy gave the man a final growl, showing her teeth as he headed toward the small, two door sports car Dolfe hadn't noticed when they pulled in. It was parked under a tree at the edge of the lot, taking advantage of some shade on a hot day.

"You need to behave yourself, Ivy," Blaise scolded. She looked at Dolfe as he opened the door. "I hope she's not going to be an ankle biter."

"Me too," Dolfe said. Then, seeing the concern in her beautiful face, Dolfe relented. "You heard Byerson. Dogs don't like him. I've met people like that. I'm sure she'll be fine."

Sure enough, as Suz spotted them entering the main room of the bar, she squealed happily and hurried over. Ivy gave Suz a delighted doggy bark and manically wagged her tail. When Blaise put her down, the little mutt bounced happily toward Suz and let herself be picked up and snuggled to within an inch of her life. "She's adorable. Where'd you get her?"

Dolfe noticed that Suz just assumed the dog was staying with them.

"She belonged to Roger White," Blaise told her friend. "She was heading to the pound."

Suz looked alarmed.

"But we rescued her," Blaise finished with a smile at Dolfe.

Stocking glasses behind the bar, Tyrese lifted a black eyebrow at Dolfe as he slid onto a tall stool.

"Don't even say it. You know the drill, Ty."

Tyrese chuckled. "Whatever Blaise wants, Blaise gets."

"Pretty much. We ran into Alex Byerson outside."

"Yeah. What a guy. He's going to lose multi-thousands of dollars covering all of *Artisan's* promised deliveries for the next week or two."

"He's making the offer to other bars?"

"I just got off the phone with William Buckert of *Willie's* down the street. Byerson offered him the same deal."

"It's certainly good PR for *Byerson's*."

Ty shook his head. "Dolfe, my man, you're way too cynical."

Dolfe shrugged. "Hazard of the job I'm afraid."

"These microbreweries are a close-knit group. I mean, sure they have a healthy competition going on, but this isn't the first time one of them has stepped in to help another brewery."

Dolfe shrugged.

Ty slid a small bowl of peanuts across the bar. "Can I get you two something to drink?"

"I'll take an iced tea," Blaise said as she slipped onto the stool next to Dolfe. She brushed her hand over her forehead, pushing damp curls away from it. "It sure is hot outside."

Suz came around the bar and grabbed a peanut bowl, dumping the peanuts into another bowl and filling it with water for Ivy. She put the bowl in front of the busily snooping dog and rubbed her hand over the soft curls on Ivy's back. "How are you doing today, girlfriend?" she asked Blaise. "I didn't expect to see you out and about."

"I'm fine." She accepted the tall iced tea Ty handed her and took a long drag off the icy drink. "Mm, that tastes good. Thanks Ty."

Suz petted Ivy for a minute and then looked up, her face folding into a frown. "I've been trying to recall more about my time in that building..."

"Did you remember something else?" Dolfe asked.

"Only the rumble of a powerful engine, like a truck or something." She straightened and leaned a hip against the bar. "I just wanted to let you know you might be looking for a big vehicle."

"Yeah. The pickup truck seems to keep popping up," Dolfe lamented.

"This guy Kopper at *Artisan* drives one, right?" Ty

asked. "He's flown the coup so it looks like he's your guy."

Dolfe sipped his water and thought about it for a minute before responding. "He certainly seems like the most obvious suspect."

"But you don't think it's him," Blaise said. It wasn't a question. She knew him too well.

"It could very well be him. I'm always just a little suspicious when things seem so straightforward. I've learned there isn't much in life that travels in such a straight line."

As if to prove his point, Ivy ran out into the middle of the bar, squatted and peed a crooked line toward the door.

Blaise shrieked and leapt off her stool, descending on the perplexed pee-er with a gentle scolding.

Ty's other eyebrow lifted and Dolfe sighed, sliding the glass of water toward Tyrese. "Give me a beer, Ty. I think I'm going to need something stronger than this."

Three pees later Dolfe found himself sitting in the waiting room at the veterinarian's office. He'd called his cousin Alastair and gotten the recommendation as they left *Tyrese's* behind and luckily the vet had an opening that afternoon.

He went to grab his cell phone to call Brita and a sheet of paper fell out onto the floor. Dolfe swore silently. With the dog drama, he'd totally forgotten the page they'd found hidden in Roger White's window shade. Retrieving the folded sheet, he opened it and frowned over the numbers and formulas written there. The content looked like something from one of Roger White's beer tests, but Dolfe wasn't enough of a scientist to interpret it.

Blaise's voice broke into his concentration and he looked up to find her walking out with another woman, a pretty brunette with dark eyes that were filled with kindness. Blaise was smiling again, looking relieved. She was holding Ivy and the dog wagged her tail, barking when she saw Dolfe.

He felt his eyes go wide. "Is that dog wearing underpants?"

"Potty pants," Blaise told him happily. Though why she'd be happy about such a development he had no clue.

"She has a UTI," the brunette told him with a grin.

He had no idea what everybody was so happy about. Whatever a UTI was it wasn't exactly producing pleasant results. First puddles every-where and now canine undergarments. He was going to be a laughingstock when his cousins got wind of this. "Unpleasant Toilet Inclinations?" he asked wryly.

Blaise gave him "the look" but doctor brunette laughed gaily.

"Basically, yes." She scratched the diminutive diaper wearer behind one enormous ear. "Poor little Ivy has a bladder infection. We've got her set up with antibiotics and she'll be right as rain in a day or two."

Dolfe stood up and grabbed his wallet. He figured he was going to be doing a lot of that in the future. "How much do we owe ya doc?"

The woman waved a hand toward the front desk, which currently had two lines of three people each. "They'll take care of you over there." She smiled at Blaise. "Now don't forget, I'll need to see Miss Ivy back in two weeks for a recheck."

"We'll be here," Blaise said, kissing her diapered charge on a wet nose. "Thanks so much."

"Anytime. It was really nice chatting with you, Blaise. Remember what I told you about..." She glanced at Dolfe. "...that other thing."

Dolfe's antennae went rigid and vibrated. "What other thing?" he asked Blaise in a harsh whisper.

She just shook her head and got in line. Ivy laid her head on Blaise's shoulder and gave him a sleepy look. Her non-droopy ear lost some of its stiffness as she fell asleep. Looking at the tiny face with the cockeyed ears, Dolfe felt something tug at his heart strings.

He quickly squelched it. Fortunately he was made of much sterner stuff than that. It would take more than a boatload of cuteness to make him fall for the little dog's act.

He hoped.

17

"Where'd you get this?" Dolfe's cousin Godric asked him.

"It's from the case I'm helping Brita with. The dead guy worked at a testing lab and we found the formula hidden in his apartment."

"Beer testing?" Godric sounded dubious.

"Yeah, why?"

A beat of silence followed, during which Dolfe was starting to get worried. "Please don't tell me we've got a bio weapon in somebody's home brew?" he asked.

"No. But it's something equally unlikely to turn up in beer."

"God, just cut to the chase. What exactly is $C_{10}H_{14}N_2$?"

"Nicotine."

Dolfe blinked. "What? Like somebody dropped their pack of cigarettes into the vat?"

"Exactly like that. Except now that I think about it, I remember reading about a microbrewery in Europe somewhere that was experimenting with adding nicotine to their beer."

Dolfe whistled. "Talk about an addictive substance. Nicotine and alcohol together..." He shook his head. "Somebody could potentially make a ton of money selling that beer."

"If they didn't kill off all their customers. Besides, they'd never get it past the FDA. The government slugs don't even want caffeine added to beer."

"I hate to agree with the government on anything but that just sounds nasty."

"Couldn't agree more. Wasn't your dead guy poisoned?"

Dolfe did a mental head slap as all the pieces fell together. "He was. Nicotine poisoning."

"That's a pretty big coincidence isn't it?"

"Too big. Thanks, man. I owe ya one."

"You can repay me by bringing Blaise over to Emma and Clovis's place on Saturday. Dini misses her. Around five?"

"Sounds great. See you then."

Dolfe disconnected and dialed Brita. She answered on the fourth ring, sounding tired. "Hey, Honeybun."

"Hey. I found something at Roger White's place."

He told her about the partial report and what he'd learned from Godric.

"That's too much of a coincidence for my comfort," Brita told him.

"My thoughts exactly."

"Hold on, I have the Medical Examiner's report here." There was a moment of silence while Dolfe pictured Brita scanning the ME's report. "The poison definitely didn't come from the e-cig. It was loaded properly. And it wasn't given to him in food. All he had in his stomach was alcohol."

"Beer?"

"Could be. Why?"

"Think about it, Brita. White tested *Artisan's* beer and failed it. Multiple times. He hides a partial report in his home showing deadly levels of nicotine and then he's murdered...poisoned with nicotine. The story nearly writes itself."

"Right now it's pure fiction. But it makes a twisted kind of sense." She paused. "You think Kopper put nicotine into White's drink?"

"Or Alvin Sparks. He was clearly working for somebody. What if Sparks was hired to take care of the Roger White problem and then whoever hired him took him out when he failed to deal properly with the other loose ends."

"Blaise and Suz."

"Yeah."

"Okay, I guess I'm looking for connections between Sparks and Kopper."

"You want me to search Sparks' place?"

"That would be a big help. Thanks, Dolfe."

"No problem. I'll let you know what I find there. If anything." He started to hang up and realized Brita was still talking. He put the phone back to his hear.

"...dog? What's her name?"

Mr. Big Mouth Alastair must have already told her about Ivy. "News sure spreads fast in this family."

"Like a wildfire during a drought. I can't believe you let Blaise get a little dog. I thought you'd hold out for some big monster like a Great Dane."

He sighed wistfully. "A man's dog. You know the drill, Brita."

"Whatever Blaise wants..."

"Blaise gets. Yeah. The dog's already been to the vet and cost me over two hundred dollars."

"Is Blaise happy?"

He shook his head, knowing where his friend was taking him. "Ecstatic. She loves the ugly little bug."

"You can't put a price tag on that, Dolfe."

He realized she was right. "We might need to get some pointers on being dog parents from you."

"Anytime. I'm an expert." She chuckled. "Bring

her to the barbeque on Saturday. I can't wait to
meet her."

She wouldn't let him off the phone until he
promised so he made the promise and hung up.

It was no bleeping wonder he felt outnumbered
all the time. He was surrounded by beautiful,
demanding women.

Then he smiled.

What in the world was he so upset about? He
might feel like he was in hell when they all ganged
up on him. But he was basically living every man's
dream.

B laise glanced at her fitness watch and
realized it was getting late. After Dolfe
dropped her off, she'd jumped into her own
car and gone out to the pet store to get Ivy the things
she'd need. That visit had taken much longer than
she'd expected because her new baby seemed to
want to say hi to everyone she came across, man,
woman, child or dog. The only exception was one
cat that was about twice Ivy's size and seemed determined to put the little dog in her place. Blaise had
also gotten Ivy's nails clipped while she was there
and spoken to the dog trainer about classes...more to
train *her* than her little dog.

Blaise finally walked out of the pet store after an

hour and a half and realized she didn't have anything for dinner that night. She took Ivy home since it was too hot to leave her in the car and headed to the grocery.

Thirty minutes later, Blaise was standing in the checkout line when she got a phone call. She didn't recognize the number and almost didn't answer. In the end, curiosity got the best of her and she accepted the call. "Hello?"

"Is this Blaise?"

"It is." Something about the voice was familiar. Blaise thought maybe she'd spoken to the woman on the other end recently.

"This is Ginny...from *Clear Brew Testing Laboratories*?"

"Ah, yes. How are you?"

"To tell you the truth, I've been better. A man was just here threatening Tabitha...my boss."

Blaise accepted her receipt from the cashier and thanked her, grabbing her cart and heading for the door. "You should really call the police, Ginny."

"He's gone and she told me she'd fire me if I called them. I didn't know what else to do. I've never seen Tab so scared. She was shaking like a leaf."

Blaise unlocked her car and dumped the bags of groceries inside. "What would you like me to do?"

"I wondered if you'd come over and talk to her, try to convince her to go to the police. I..." There was a tension-filled pause. "I'm really afraid he means to hurt her."

Remembering how arrogant and self-assured Tabitha Clear was, Blaise doubted the woman would listen to her. But she might be able to get some information on who was threatening the owner of Clear labs. There was a good chance it was connected to the murders. "I'll be there in about twenty minutes. I need to stop home and unload some groceries first."

"Good. Thanks so much, Blaise."

As she was pulling into their driveway, Blaise dialed Dolfe up and quickly told him what Ginny had told her. "I think I should talk to Tabitha. Maybe it was Kopper and she can tell us where he's gone."

"Are you sure he's gone?" Dolfe asked.

"Ginny said he was, yes."

"Okay, then you're right. It would be good to get a description and try to find out what Miss Clear might have done to make him so mad. But if there's any sign of danger...even a sniff of it...get Ginny and Tabitha out of there. Bring them home and I'll join you. Apparently whatever's going on, *Clear Brew Labs* is mixed up in it. Even beyond Roger's involvement."

"I'll call you after my visit." Blaise disconnected and hurried into the house. Ivy met her at the door and followed her through the house, bouncing happily at her heels. She quickly set the little dog up with a bed next to theirs in the bedroom and water and food dishes in the kitchen.

Blaise put her groceries away and, before she left for *Clear Brew Laboratories*, she grabbed her can of mace from the fruit bowl where she kept it. She was going to be prepared for whatever came her way.

18

D olfe tried to make his way through some paperwork but was having trouble concentrating. Somehow his array of cases, from tracking a possibly cheating spouse, to trying to uncover an exotic animal ring in the city, couldn't keep his interest over an unsolved case of murder and abduction.

Especially when Blaise was spreading her investigative wings and unwittingly putting herself into dangerous situations. He knew she was smart and had proven herself capable of getting out of some of the dangerous scrapes she'd found herself in, but she was a breath away from full-on disaster at any given moment.

It was giving him gray hairs.

His phone rang and he answered it quickly, hoping it was Blaise calling to ask him to come with.

Instead, it was a client for whom he'd recently solved a case of employee theft. Unfortunately, the case hadn't been as cut and dried as he'd hoped. It turned out the employee was stealing food from the family owned restaurant to give to a group of homeless people down the street.

Since the restaurant's owner wasn't interested in feeding that particular group of people because they'd defaced his property and harassed his customers weeks earlier, the discovery was sure to end the employee's career at the diner.

Dolfe had mixed feelings about that.

He quickly gave the client his report, doing his best to soften the employee's motives, but he was pretty sure the pretty twenty-something redhead who'd worked for the diner since leaving high school would be on the streets herself soon, looking for another job.

Unless the diner's owner pressed charges. Then, Dolfe was afraid he'd be faced with a conundrum. He'd feel compelled to testify on the employee's behalf. Especially since she'd been eschewing her own tips to pay for the food she took.

By the time he hung up, Dolfe was so distracted by his thoughts he barely heard his office door open.

When he looked up, it took him a beat to realize who he was looking at. By the time he recognized David Kopper, it was too late to react to the gun the man was holding.

B laise entered the door marked with a wood and brass sign that read, *Clear Brew Testing Laboratories*. Ginny wasn't in the lobby when she entered. Blaise stood there for a moment, thinking, and then remembered that Ginny had been pretty creeped out by the guy who'd fought with her boss. Maybe she was hiding somewhere waiting for Blaise. Or maybe she'd gone back into Tabitha Clear's office to try to talk her into calling the police again.

Blaise didn't relish the idea of facing off with Tabitha. Besides, she didn't know how to explain her presence there without implicating the concerned receptionist, so she slipped down the hallway and headed for the break room where she and Ginny had chatted before. It seemed the logical place to look for the other woman.

Unfortunately Ginny wasn't there. Blaise ducked into the ladies room and found it empty too. On an impulse, she did a quick check of the men's room, with no better luck.

She stepped back into the hallway, her gaze sliding reluctantly toward Tabitha's office, and sighed. It looked like she had no choice. She was going to have to speak to Tabitha. It was just as well, maybe the woman would listen to sense from her where she'd ignored her employee.

Blaise was reaching for the knob when the door opened and she found herself staring into Ginny's stricken face.

"Oh, there you are. I've been looking..." Blaise's gaze slipped downward, to Ginny's hands, which she was holding out to her sides. They were covered in blood and she was vibrating with emotion. "Oh my god, Ginny," Blaise exclaimed. "Are you all right?"

The woman shook her head, her eyes glassy. "He..." A sob escaped. "He killed her, Blaise."

The door swung back on its hinges and Blaise looked past Ginny.

Tabitha Clear lay in a crumpled pile in front of her desk, a puddle of blood spreading away from her body.

Blaise swallowed hard, her mind spinning. "Okay, we need to call the police."

Ginny shook her head, her eyes wide. "They'll think I killed her!"

Blaise frowned, her finger hovering over the final 1 of 911. "Why on earth would they think that?"

Tears slid down Ginny's face. She shook her head and lifted a bloody hand toward her face. She stopped, frowning at the blood, and then sobbed again. "Because I'm the only one here. Who else would they blame?"

"When did you see the man and Tabitha arguing? How long ago?"

"I don't know, an hour maybe?"

"Did anybody else see him?"

"No!" she exclaimed, clearly frustrated. "Everyone else was gone."

"What about security cameras?"

Ginny sniffed loudly. "Not in the office. We're just a brew lab. Why would we need security cameras in here?"

"Outside in the halls?"

Ginny shrugged. "Maybe. But there's no need to look at them. I know who killed her."

Blaise didn't bother to explain to the distraught woman that the cameras would corroborate her story, if not clear her altogether. She'd give her time to settle down and start thinking again. "Who was it, Ginny? Who was Tabitha arguing with?"

Ginny blinked. "Oh, didn't I tell you?"

"No," Blaise said, striving for calm. "You didn't."

"Oh, sorry. It was a client. That's how I know him. Though I haven't seen him very many times. Tabitha introduced us once, and sometimes he brings in the samples to be tested. If he's going to be in the area or something." Ginny sniffed again and cocked her head. "Personally, I think he was sweet on Tab."

Blaise sighed. "Ginny. The name?"

"Gosh. I'm a hot mess. Sorry. Kopper. David Kopper."

Dolfe lifted his hands, his gaze locked on Kopper even as his mind started to look for solutions to his little gun problem. The man fixed Dolfe with a jittery blue gaze. "I don't want to hurt you."

"Well, that's good to hear. Then you won't mind if I put my arms down." Dolfe slowly lowered his hands, placing them on top of his desk.

Kopper jerked as if someone had smacked him. "I only want to set the record straight."

"You can do that without the gun, Mr. Kopper."

Kopper's twitchy gaze slid to the gun clutched in his oversized hand. He looked at it as if he'd forgotten it was there. "I wasn't sure if you'd listen to me. I can't go to jail."

Dolfe nodded, his hand sliding slowly toward his cell phone. "Okay, that's a place to start. Why don't you lower the gun and have a seat, Mr. Kopper. Tell me what's going on and, if I can, I'll help you."

Kopper didn't sit. The gun stayed focused on a swath of Dolfe that included his left ear to his right elbow. The brewery manager was shaking so badly he could barely hold the gun still. "Nobody can help me."

"Then why are you here?"

The man jerked again and blinked. Clearly his intentions and his motor skills were living in different zip codes. "I didn't know what else to do."

Dolfe's fingertips found his cell. He hesitated, giving Kopper a neutral look. "I can't help if you don't tell me what's going on."

Kopper shook his head. Sweat beaded his upper lip and turned the bright red curls along his hairline auburn. "I'm being set up."

Dolfe barely managed to keep his expression blank. He'd yet to meet a crook who didn't try the "I've been set up" defense. "Who's setting you up?"

Kopper gave his head a jerk. "If I tell you that you'll give them a heads up. They'll kill me."

"Not if you're in jail." As soon as the words left Dolfe's mouth he regretted them.

Kopper twitched several times as if he'd stepped on a live wire in a puddle of water and the gun stopped moving. It focused right between Dolfe's eyes. Kopper's lips curled back from yellowed teeth and his beady blue eyes went hard. "I told you, Mr. Honeybun, I can't go to jail."

Dolfe hit a button on his phone and prayed Kopper wouldn't hear Brita's voice when she answered. He spoke quickly to distract the other man. "And I told you I'd help, Kopper. But you need to trust me. You can't come in here and point a gun at me and expect my help. It doesn't work that way."

Kopper gave that a moment's thought and then nodded. "I'll tell you this. I was being blackmailed. I'm not exactly sure who it was. I've been trying to figure that out. I was pretty sure Tabitha Clear was behind it. But I don't know anymore."

"Why would the owner of *Clear Brew Labs* blackmail you?"

Kopper's gaze narrowed and slid guiltily away. "I..." He shook his head. "I didn't do anything illegal. People love our beers. They can't get enough of them."

"If that's true, it sounds like it might be a problem with the competition."

His eyes went wide as if he hadn't considered that. "You think one of the other brewers is behind all this?"

"All what, Mr. Kopper?"

Kopper's long frame sucked back and folded as if he wanted to disappear. "Me being blackmailed. Roger White getting killed."

Dolfe's pulse sped. The police had never released the information that White was murdered. As far as the public knew, he'd died of accidental nicotine poisoning. "How do you know White was killed?" Dolfe kept his tone as calm as he could. He didn't want to spook Kopper into doing anything radical.

Still, the man's small blue eyes narrowed as he realized the trap he'd set for himself. "White shouldn't have gone after *Artisan*. It wasn't right. Our products are safe and popular. We were on track to come out on top. Now we'll be lucky to survive."

"That sounds like a powerful motive to kill Roger

White," Dolfe said softly. To his surprise, Kopper laughed.

"It does, doesn't it?" He laughed harder, his pale face turning red. "Oh god, I can't believe I've gotten myself into this mess. How did this happen?"

A siren flared in the distance and Dolfe prayed Brita had enough sense to cut it before she pulled up in front of his building. But it grew continually louder until it flashed past and continued on.

Body rigid with alarm, Kopper went to the window and watched the squad car fly past. When he turned back, Dolfe had the drawer open and his hand on his weapon. He never got a chance to fire.

Kopper reacted much more quickly than Dolfe could have imagined.

19

*B*laise nodded. "We think Kopper killed Roger White." She leaned against the ladies room counter and watched Ginny wash blood from her hands.

Ginny frowned. "Well, he's certainly angry enough to have killed Roger. But I have no idea why."

"My understanding is that Roger had scored *Artisan's* last few tests badly."

"I wouldn't know anything about that. I'm just the receptionist."

"It apparently cost *Artisan* a lot of money. That would make Kopper mad, right?"

Ginny frowned, reaching for a paper towel to dry her hands. "I guess. But batches fail all the time. If brewers killed the scientists for that we'd have been out of business long ago."

"Unless Roger thought there was something else going on."

Ginny's eyes went wide. She pushed the Ladies room door open and turned to Blaise. "I think I might know what." Her touch, when she grasped Blaise's hand, was cool and damp. "I'm pretty sure I heard Kopper say the word 'blackmail' when he was yelling at Tab. "Do you suppose Roger and Tab were blackmailing him over his results and that's why he killed them?"

"That's certainly plausible." Blaise looked at her phone. "I really need to call the police. They have to process the crime scene and you need to tell them what you know."

Ginny nodded, stopping beside her desk. "I agree. But can you let me call them? I owe that to Tab."

"Sure." Blaise was relieved. "You're right. You found her so you should call."

Ginny sat down and put her head in her hands. She was clearly distraught. Her hands were visibly shaking.

Blaise patted her on the back. "You okay?"

"Yeah. I just need a minute." She looked up. "Could I be alone. Would you mind?"

"Not at all. I'll just go to the breakroom and grab a coffee. You want anything?"

"No. But thanks."

Blaise moved down the hall, her gaze sliding to

Tabitha Clear's office door. She stopped, staring at the door for a long moment. She really shouldn't. Dolfe would give her an earful if he found out. But then that had never stopped her before.

And she wouldn't get such a great opportunity again.

Her mind made up, she glanced back toward Ginny and saw her speaking softly on the phone, her head still in her hands.

Blaise figured she had about five minutes before Ginny hung up. She'd tell the other woman afterward. She wasn't going to disturb anything. But maybe there was something in Tabitha's office that would tie Kopper to Roger White's murder.

Blaise didn't examine her reasons beyond that. She knew Brita was a very good detective. And she had a Crime Scene Unit behind her that really knew its stuff. But once the evidence was collected, she and Dolfe wouldn't get a chance at it unless Brita decided to share.

Blaise had nearly died because of the Roger White case. She figured she had a right to know what was going on. Conscience duly soothed, Blaise pulled her sleeve over her hand and twisted the door knob, pushing the door into the room. She slipped through and nudged it quietly closed behind her.

The sickly sweet scent of fresh death assailed her nostrils. Blaise covered her nose with her hand and closed her eyes, fighting the urge to turn and run.

After a long moment she forced herself to move. She gazed down at Tabitha Clear, finding her surprisingly beautiful even in death. The woman's hair was still perfectly twisted into the business like but still feminine knot at the back of her head. Her business suit was pink, the white tank beneath spattered with blood. One of her tan pumps was beneath the desk, the other still on her long, narrow foot. She lay on her side, arms outstretched and fingers spread as if she'd been trying to protect herself from the attacker. The pool of blood beneath her head was darkening as it aged and dried.

Blaise felt a thrum of sadness. Such a young, beautiful woman...by all accounts a smart business woman...vital and alive one minute and gone the next.

It made Blaise want to embrace her blessings and strive to improve at the same time. She shook off the melancholy and moved around Tabitha's desk, taking care not to touch anything. She examined the tidy surface of the desk and the long dresser behind it. There were three pictures on the dresser. One of Tabitha with a young boy, too old to be a son so presumably her brother. One of Tabitha in a kayak, the horizon filled with rocky cliffs and water sparkling around her. The third picture was of her standing at the center of a group, a trophy in her hands and a wide smile on her face. Blaise recognized some of the microbrewers around her. David

Kopper was there, Kopper's assistant whose name they never got, Alex Byerson, and several others Blaise didn't recognize. No Roger. The picture must have been taken before he started working at *Clear Brew*. Or he was the one taking the picture. Everyone was smiling and a crowd of people and equipment behind them gave the picture a convention feel. She made a note to ask Ginny where it had been taken.

She pulled her sleeve over her hand again and tugged drawers and a pair of center doors open, finding some personal stuff in the drawers and booze in the center cabinet. Blaise was just about to close the last drawer when she spotted several small, clear bottles with bright blue lids. She pushed a scarf to the side and extracted one of the bottles, frowning.

It was e-liquid. Like the kind Roger White would have used in his e-cigarette. Could he have been poisoned with a bottle like the one she held in her hand? And if so, did that mean Tabitha poisoned her own scientist?

"Blaise?"

She whipped around at the sound of Ginny's voice and was still holding the tiny bottle when the door swung open.

Ginny frowned at her. "What are you doing?"

"I was just seeing if I could figure out what happened to Tab."

"It's pretty obvious isn't it? Somebody bashed her over the head with that." Ginny pointed to a bloody trophy lying on its side a few feet away from the body. Blaise recognized it as the trophy Tabitha had been holding in the photo.

"Right." Blaise didn't want to admit she hadn't even seen the trophy. "But maybe the killer left something behind."

Ginny's expression turned suspicious. "In Tab's drawer?"

Lifting the tiny bottle, Blaise asked, "Why did Tabitha have several bottles of e-liquid in her drawer?"

"She was trying to quit. Both of them were, in fact, her and Roger." Ginny smiled sadly. "Things were a bit tense around here at first with both of them quitting."

"I'll bet." Blaise slipped the bottle back inside the drawer and closed it, giving Ginny a guilty smile. "Sorry for snooping. I didn't find anything useful anyway."

Ginny's narrowed gaze told Blaise her new friend didn't believe her. "You'd tell me if you did, right?"

"Of course. I do have a question though. That picture there...the one on the end...where was that taken?"

"Oh, that was last year's Micro-Brewer's Conference." She gave Blaise a proud smile. "*Clear Brew* was voted best Brew Lab in the state." Her gaze slid to the bloody trophy. "Tab was really proud of that award."

"I noticed Roger wasn't in the picture."

"No, he wouldn't be. It was only for owners and principles. Regular employees were manning the booths."

The front door jangled and Ginny's head snapped around. "That will be the police. You coming?"

Blaise hurried after the receptionist, closing the door behind her and trying to melt into the woodwork as they entered the lobby. The last thing she wanted Brita to know was that she'd been snooping around her crime scene.

But it wasn't Brita who was waiting for them when they reached the lobby. The newcomer and Brita did have one thing in common, the woman holding the gun on Blaise didn't appear happy to see her. In fact, she looked downright angry.

She cocked her head and scowled, lifting the gun toward Blaise and Ginny. "I knew you were going to be trouble the moment I laid eyes on you."

Blaise made a small sound of surprise and, before she even realized what she was doing, stepped in front of Ginny. "You don't want to shoot us. The police are on their way right now. They should be here any moment."

The woman laughed, tilting her head to address the woman behind Blaise. "Is that true, Ginny? Did you call the police?"

Blaise waited for Ginny's affirmative response.

Instead, what she got was a sharp sting on her neck and a dark chuckle from behind. "Nope. I just made the one call." From the corner of her eye, Blaise could just make out the syringe Ginny was holding against her throat.

"Well...then I guess that was to me." Blaise's attention was wrenched away from Ginny and drawn back to David Kopper's assistant. The middle-aged woman smiled.

Blaise shuddered at the chilling sight.

D olfe ducked the flying gun and lifted his own weapon. He aimed it at the sobbing man across the room. "I can't believe you threw your gun at me."

Kopper ran a hand beneath his eyes, sniffling. "I don't want to shoot anybody. In fact I have no idea *how* to shoot. That thing probably isn't even loaded. I just needed some leverage to make you listen to me."

Dolfe realized he wouldn't need his gun and lowered it. Placing it on top of his desk, he jerked his head toward Kopper. "Take a seat, Mr. Kopper. Tell me what's going on."

The other man ran a long-fingered hand through bright red curls. He looked down his nose at Dolfe, his small eyes shiny with unshed tears. "I'm ruined.

Nobody will buy *Artisan Beers* after this and I'll be fired for sure."

"What have you done?"

Kopper's bony legs bent at the knees and he collapsed into a chair under the window. Behind him, the sky was abloom with a beautiful sunset, the colors turning his clownish hair an even brighter red and washing his features to white. "I was just trying to create a beer my customers couldn't resist. It isn't technically illegal. Not yet, anyway. And for a while it seemed to be working. Habitude is our biggest seller. As I'd hoped, people couldn't seem to get enough of it."

Dolfe remembered Nathan Lord talking about that beer. Saying much the same thing about it. "Go on."

Kopper sighed, lowering his head. "Caffeine."

Dolfe felt his eyes go wide. "You added caffeine to the beer?"

"Early trials haven't been very promising. Beer brewed with coffee beans had too strong a flavor and people didn't like the idea of it. I used a special bean and a unique process that didn't leave the bitter flavor behind. My process is genius. I just knew it would be popular. And I was right."

"Then what's the problem?"

Kopper shook his head. "The FDA is in the process of restricting caffeine use in beer. If they knew about Habitude they'd stop us from selling it or worse."

"How in the world did you expect to float it past them?"

Kopper lifted his head, looking proudly defiant. "Big ideas are often unpopular at first, Mr. Honeybun. Once I knew it was popular I'd planned to go to them and admit to testing my process. After showing them a safe, delicious product I'd hoped to talk them into letting us sell it."

"Why did Roger White have a copy of the Habitude test results showing dangerous levels of nicotine?"

Kopper barely reacted, telling Dolfe he'd known about the report. Shaking his head, Kopper started to pace the room. "That man had it out for me. He probably doctored the sample."

"Why would he have it out for you, Mr. Kopper?"

"Simple. Before he started working at *Clear Brew* he tried to get a job in our brew lab. I wouldn't hire him."

"Why not?"

Kopper shrugged. "Something about him rubbed me the wrong way, Mr. Honeybun. I didn't trust him."

"He seemed to fail your samples a lot. More than any other brewer. Why did you keep going to *Clear Brew* with them?"

"Mr. Sands insisted on using *Clear Brew Labs*. He was friends with Tabitha's parents and he trusted and liked her. As often as possible I'd request one of the other scientists. But occasionally I still got White."

"If you didn't trust White, why did you send him a sample of a beer you knew could get *Artisan* into trouble?"

Bushy, red eyebrows peaked. "I didn't send him samples of Habitude. At least not the caffeinated beer. I sent him samples without the special ingredient."

Shaking his head, Dolfe sat back in his chair. "Sounds highly unethical. And I wonder why you'd even bother testing the doctored sample."

Kopper's head snapped up and his expression was fiercely proud. "There are many things to test for, Mr. Honeybun. CO_2, gluten, protein, sediment, or microbiological analyses. The list is long. *Artisan Beers* is very proud of our products and we work hard at making sure we're selling the best craft and microbrews in the market."

"Your story is that someone at *Clear Brew* added nicotine to the sample?"

Kopper curled his lip. "You tell me. I sent them a clean sample and the next day I received a call telling me White found deadly amounts of nicotine in it and was going to go to the FDA with his report if I didn't step down and pay up."

"Roger White called to threaten you?" Dolfe asked, frowning.

Kopper shook his head. "I didn't recognize the voice. But I promptly got White on the phone and told him I wouldn't let him blackmail me. I wish you could have heard him crow when I confronted him. He denied being part of the blackmail of course, but he was clearly happy to have found something to use against me. He had to have been part of it."

"If Roger White and Tabitha were blackmailing you, then why did Roger end up dead?"

"Who knows? There's no honor among thieves. Maybe he tried to cross Tabitha. I always thought that woman was a shark."

So much for a small, close-knit community, Dolfe thought. "Okay, so you packaged up the doctored sample..."

"Not doctored, Mr. Honeybun. Simply sans caffeine."

"A distinction without a difference, Mr. Kopper. What happened after you packaged it up?"

"Georgina took it to the lab."

"Georgina?"

"My assistant." Kopper flushed. "Technically, she's not my assistant. She's been with *Artisan* since its beginnings five years ago. She's a stockholder who wanted to stay involved in the day to day business so the owner asked her if she'd like to help me manage."

Warning bells rang in Dolfe's brain. "Georgina didn't want to manage the business herself?"

"If she did, she's never said anything to me."

"Would she say something to you? I mean, you were selected over her. It seems to me that she'd be reluctant to let you know how much she'd wanted the job."

Kopper shrugged. "Artie didn't think she was smart enough to run the business. I tended to agree."

"Artie is the owner?" Dolfe asked.

"Yeah."

"Why didn't he want her to run *Artisan Beers*?"

"Probably because she's got anger issues. She used to be in the FBI and has a bit of a God complex to go with it. Not a good combination."

Rage, training, and a tactical mind...Just the kind of person they were looking for. "I noticed a bit of tension between you and Georgina when I was there. Maybe she resented that you got the position she wanted. Maybe she's been looking for a way to get even. Maybe turning in a dosed sample was her way."

Kopper frowned. "I can see her doing that. She's kind of a b..." He glanced at Dolfe. "Anyway, yeah. I could see that."

"Can you see her killing to cover it up?"

"But that doesn't compute. Why would she give *Clear Brew Labs* a tainted sample and then kill the lab tech to cover it up?"

"Maybe the goal wasn't to take Artisan down, but to punish you. If Roger White went to the FDA that would harm Artisan too, wouldn't it?"

Kopper's eyes went wide. "That actually makes sense."

Dolfe thought Kopper agreed too readily to the potential scenario he'd laid out. But he was starting to understand how some of the pieces fit together. There was just one more detail.

"Mr. Kopper, does Georgina know a guy named Alvin Sparks?"

"I have no idea. Should she?"

"If she's involved in the murders, yes."

Kopper scrunched up his long face, parodying a thinking man. After a moment he said. "She has a nephew named Al. I guess that could be him."

Dolfe grabbed his phone and called Brita. When she answered he didn't waste time on pleasantries. "Brit, do a background on Alvin Sparks and Georgina..." He suddenly realized he didn't know her last name. He glanced at Kopper.

"Sands. Her husband's name is Art, thus the name *Artisan*." Kopper screwed up his face to show what he thought of that.

"Her husband owns *Artisan Beers*?"

"Well yeah. I thought you knew that."

Dolfe shook his head. "Last name Sands. From where I sit she's got a solid motive. It looks like she's been framing Kopper. We just need to tie her to Sparks. And see what kind of vehicle she drives."

Brita promised to get the information and get back to him.

Dolfe hung up and stood. "I'm going to *Artisan* to talk to Mrs. Sands. I want you to head over to IMPD Headquarters on King. Ask for Detective Brita Muldane and answer any questions she asks you. With any luck we'll have you cleared of this mess by tonight."

Kopper stood. "Sure. If it will get me out of this it will be my pleasure."

Dolfe nodded, grabbed his gun and keys and headed for the door.

"Mr. Honeybun."

He stopped, turning back.

"I don't think Georgina's at the office. I was just there and she was gone."

"Do you know where she might be?"

"This time of night I'd expect her to be at home."

"Do you have that number?"

Dolfe typed the phone number in as Kopper recited it to him. The phone rang several times before it was finally picked up by a woman with an Hispanic accent. "Yes?"

"My name is Honeybun. I need to speak to Mrs. Sands please?"

"I'm sorry, Meester Honeybuns, Meezus Sands es not here."

"I'm working with the police and it's very important that I speak to her. Do you know where she might be?"

"She say someteen about an errand. I'm sorry I can't help."

"Do you know her cell phone number?"

"Yes, but I..."

"Police business, ma'am."

"Yes, sir. Of course."

The woman gave him the number and Dolfe quickly dialed it. It went to voicemail. He ushered Kopper out of his office and locked the door, heading quickly toward his truck. Dialing Brita again, Dolfe asked her to trace the phone.

Moments later, as he was heading across town toward *Artisan Beers*, Brita came back on the line. "I have that information for you, Dolfe. Sparks *is* Georgina Sands's nephew. And she drives a light gray Dodge pickup truck. Looks like she's our killer."

Dolfe smiled. "Got her. What about her location?"

"Oh, sorry, right now she's at *Clear Brew Labs*."

His pulse spiked and his stomach did a painful little flip. Dolfe slammed his palm on the steering wheel, swearing.

"What's wrong?" Brita asked.

"Blaise is at *Clear Brew*." He jammed his foot down on the gas, taking the next turn on two, wildly squealing tires.

"I'll meet you there," Brita told him before disconnecting.

"Hurry, Brit," Dolfe murmured as he let the phone drop to his lap.

The light in front of him turned yellow well before he reached the intersection but Dolfe laid on his horn and gunned through it. He almost hoped there was a traffic cop nearby. Given what the murderous Georgina had already done, he figured he could probably use some backup.

20

*B*laise kept her gaze averted from the gun as if that would make it go away. She held very still to keep the needle at her throat from piercing skin. With two potentially deadly problems to tackle, she decided to address the one closest to taking her down. She shifted her gaze sideways to address Ginny. "What's in the syringe?"

The other woman lifted her hand to show Blaise a tiny bottle. "Apparently you were snooping around in Tabitha's office and accidently broke this bottle of nicotine all over your skin. I'm afraid it was a fatal mistake."

Blaise's heartrate picked up and she felt sick. "You're going to inject me with the stuff and pour the e-liquid in the bottle over my hands and arms."

Ginny shifted sideways so she could look into

Blaise's face. "Smart girl. Too bad you had to get so nosy. I really kind of liked you."

"Cut the pleasantries and let's get this done," the older woman said.

Blaise looked the woman in the eyes, trying to appeal to her humanity. Unfortunately, the other woman didn't seem to have any. "You killed Tabitha Clear?"

The woman laughed. "Me? No, that would be the woman holding the deadly syringe to your throat."

Blaise looked at Ginny. "Why?"

"Why did I kill Tab and why will I kill you? That's simple. I'm tired of being treated like I'm stupid. I have almost the same training Roger did, but Tab didn't think I could do the work." Ginny's smile was mean. "I guess I proved her wrong. It was me who added the fatal amount of nicotine to the sample Georgina brought in. Roger never even guessed the sample had been tampered with."

"But what was the point?" Blaise asked. She had to keep the two women talking until she saw a chance to stop them. Or until her honey figured out she was in trouble and came riding in on his white horse. Unfortunately, she knew the chances of that were slim to none. She'd have to get out of the current mess all by herself.

"Career enhancement," the older woman said. "We've both been shoved into jobs that are beneath us. Underrated and underutilized. Nobody was going to give us a break so we're giving ourselves one."

"A shotgun promotion, if you will," Ginny said on a laugh.

"Exactly," the other woman said, laughing huskily. "I like that."

"You framed Kopper?" Blaise asked, her mind spinning. Maybe if she ducked away from the needle and dove behind Ginny's desk... But she had no idea what she'd do after that.

"He was such an easy target," his assistant said. "As soon as Al called and told him he was going down because of Roger's findings, he panicked and made himself look even more guilty by running. Then it was just a matter of stashing Alvin's van in front of Kopper's place and tying up a few loose ends."

Anger flared. "Those loose ends were my friends."

The woman shrugged. "Dierdre should have stayed out of it."

"Roger planned to tell her about the nicotine," Ginny supplied helpfully. "He wasn't sure what to do and he figured, since she'd been in the business for years she might be able to help him figure it out."

"But they never even met that night," Blaise argued. "You didn't need to try to kill her."

"We weren't sure what he'd told her," Ginny shrugged. "It was safer."

In that moment Blaise realized how truly cold blooded the two women were. "What about Suz? Why'd you kidnap her?"

The older woman gave a long-suffering sigh. "Alvin made a mess of that. He was supposed to kill her and be done with it. But he wobbled on me. He wanted to try for some ransom money."

"So you killed him too," Blaise said in a defeated voice. If she didn't figure something out fast she was going to die.

The woman shrugged. "It was him or me. And trust me, his loss will not be felt by anybody."

Blaise shook her head, disgusted.

"Your friend, Suz, was in the wrong place at the wrong time," Ginny said. "If she'd gotten hold of the vial of e-liquid I'd poisoned Roger with she might have given it to the police. I couldn't risk that. My prints were on that vial."

Blaise couldn't resist a dig. "That was pretty careless."

Ginny shrugged. "I couldn't very well wear latex gloves in the bar. Roger would have probably wondered why I was wearing a glove when I sat down to chat." She laughed gaily as if she'd told a splendid joke.

"If the vial had prints, why'd you leave it there?"

"I didn't leave it on purpose. I dropped it and it got kicked down the hall. Then Dierdre showed up and I had to get out of there fast. Unfortunately, when I came to retrieve it the next day your friend almost caught me."

The air conditioning kicked on and Blaise jumped, earning herself a painful stick with the syringe. She could tell the woman with the gun was getting restless so she hurried to keep them talking. "Which one of you killed poor Nathan?"

Kopper's assistant frowned. "That was too bad, really. He was just a young, stupid kid." She shrugged. "But he spotted Kopper sneaking into that old warehouse to drop the money we'd demanded. I didn't know any way to avoid killing him at that point."

Blaise tried to hide her shock. "You? It was you who knocked me out?"

The woman's lips thinned, her broad shoulders went square and her body tightened with rage. "You see, that's the reaction I'm so tired of. I was in government service for years. I know how to fight. I'm not some old woman with a walker you know."

The force of the woman's quick rage was frightening and Blaise suddenly wished she'd kept her mouth shut. "I'm just surprised because I thought you were a man..."

When the woman's face turned white Blaise wanted to kick herself. She'd jumped right from the frying pan into a raging fire.

"Enough chatter. She's trying to stall us," Ginny's friend said. "Do it."

Ginny looked Blaise in the eye. "Sorry, sister." Then she Jammed the syringe into Blaise's throat. Blaise jerked away before the other woman could depress the plunger, swinging a leg out and stabbing Ginny in the shin with her heel.

Ginny cried out and let go of the syringe just as the gun went off.

Blaise dove behind a chair and yanked the syringe out. The bullet missed her by inches, drilling a hole into the wall behind her.

Ginny was on her feet again and rushing her as the office door slammed back into the wall and the gun toting brewery assistant swung around, firing wildly.

Then Blaise forgot what was going on by the door because Ginny was on her and she was reaching for the syringe.

Blaise held it away from her body as Ginny grappled for it, howling with rage as Blaise's longer arms kept it away. Finally, the young woman clamped a surprisingly strong hand around Blaise's wrist and tried to push the needle toward Blaise's throat again.

Blaise didn't have the arm strength to hold her off and the needle was getting close. Too close. Ginny was going to win and Blaise would die.

With help only feet away.

In desperation, Blaise kicked at the chair legs, slamming it into Ginny just as the needle found

Blaise's skin again. It ripped across her throat, tearing flesh as it went.

The tip broke off somewhere along the way but Ginny went down to her side and Blaise did the only thing she knew to do. She jammed the needle into Ginny's thigh and hit the plunger, taking care to only push it halfway.

The woman screamed, lunging for the syringe and Blaise scampered away. She came up against a hard chest and a firm embrace as familiar arms wrapped around her.

"Are you all right, Beautiful?"

She looked up into Dolfe's worried gaze and nodded. "We need to get her to a doctor. I injected her with e-liquid. She'll die."

Brita grabbed Ginny's wildly flailing arms and threw her to the ground on her belly, quickly cuffing her wrists.

"We'll take care of it," Brita told Blaise. "Are you all right?"

Blaise nodded, rubbing her arms. "I've had just about enough of these two though."

"I hear you. You've been through a lot over the last couple of days." Brita jerked Ginny to her feet. "Why don't you go home. It'll take me half the night to sort this out and process these two. I can talk to you about all this in the morning."

Blaise didn't argue. She was thrilled to be leaving the horrible place and was halfway to the door, where uniform cops had the other woman cuffed and on her knees, bleeding from a wound on her arm, before she remembered Tabitha.

She jerked to a stop, looking up at Dolfe. "Honeybun, as much as I'd love to go home with you right now, I think I'm going to be needed here."

He looked a question but didn't argue as Blaise turned to Brita and announced, "There's been another murder..."

21

*C*haos. Pure, unadulterated chaos. In honor of Ivy's addition to the family, Brita brought her little red, long-haired dachshund, Moxie, to the barbeque, Alastair brought his doxie, Jaws, and Alf brought his big, shaggy monster, Clancy to join the fun. Darth Dane, Clovis and Emma's Great Dane puppy and the youngest member of the family, bounced from person to person, using a goofy grin and wildly flopping ears to extort bits of food that seemed to do nothing but increase his puppy appetite.

Though she started out the day like a helicopter pet mom, Blaise had given up trying to keep little Ivy, who seemed to think it was grand fun running in happy circles with the other dogs, out of harm's way.

Truth be known, it was the sight of Ivy reducing the hundred pound Clancy to a quivering pile of regret with a single, high-pitched yip that finally allowed her to fall, exhausted into a chair.

Dolfe handed her an icy drink and she looked up at him gratefully. "I might not survive this."

He laughed. "She's fine, Mama. Look at her."

And indeed little Miss Ivy *was* fine. She was currently holding court in the shade, a paw-shaped frozen watermelon treat between her tiny paws as she snuggled against Clancy's belly. Jaws and Moxie worked on their own icy treats and Clancy stared at them all with sad eyes, his head resting on his tree-trunk sized legs. He'd devoured his treat without even chewing. Darth was two inches away, his big nose quivering as he eyed Ivy's treat with happy anticipation. It was clear the giant sized baby was only waiting for an inattentive moment to snatch the little dog's treat. But the occasional stink eye and frequent growls coming from the ten pound mutt with ears bigger than she was kept him from making his move.

"Blaise!"

Blaise turned with a grin to find Godric's honey, Dini bearing down on her with open arms. She stood up and accepted a hug from her friend. "How are you, girlfriend? You look beautiful."

Dini tugged a midnight black strand of hair off her damp cheek and rolled her eyes. "It's hotter than blazes and I'm sick of Summer already."

Ivy jumped up and ran over to greet the

newcomer. Darth Dane dove on her unfinished treat, happily swallowing it whole and then giving Clancy a smug grin before flopping back down in the shade, his work done.

Ivy greeted Dini with a series of high-pitched barks, her enormous ears waggling as she wriggled her butt with canine happiness.

Dini's face lit up. "Oh, there she is!" She started to reach for Ivy and stopped, looking at Blaise. "Is it okay?"

Blaise settled herself back in her lounge chair. "Of course. She loves to be held."

"The little rat's spoiled rotten already," Dolfe told Dini. But as the Native American beauty lifted his new charge into her arms and snuggled her, securing lots of doggy kisses in return, Dolfe found himself grinning proudly.

Blaise caught his gaze and winked, her own smile filled with contentment.

"Where's Godric," Dolfe asked, to change the subject.

Dini rubbed her nose against Ivy's and giggled as a small pink tongue found her chin. "Playing football in the side yard. I've been given orders to show up for my position assignment so I'm hiding out."

Dolfe shook his head. "It's too hot for football."

Dini sighed. "Tell the rest of the Honeybuns that." She settled Ivy back on the ground and the little dog ran directly back to her new pack.

A tiny shadow fell over Blaise's chair. "Can I hold, Ivy, pleathe?" Pricilla Banks asked Blaise. Her mama, Emma, waved as Blaise glanced her way, nodding that it was okay with her. Blaise hesitated a beat, probably not wanting Ivy to fail her first child experience by nipping at or bossing the adorable little girl and scaring her. But the newly turned six-year-old batted beautiful golden brown eyes at Blaise and placed her tiny hands on Blaise's knees, imploring her with the cutest face Dolfe had ever seen.

Blaise was putty in the child's hands. "You sure can." She whistled and all five dogs' heads jerked up. "Come here, Miss Ivy."

Ivy stood and turned, tail wagging as she barked happily in response. Dolfe saw the problem right away and grinned. Unfortunately, he didn't think Blaise realized her mistake until all five dogs were bounding in her direction, tongues lolling and tails wagging with excitement.

Blaise gave a little squeal and grabbed Cilla, pulling her onto her lap to protect her as the drooling canine pack thundered down on them.

Dolfe stepped in front of the chair to cut them off. Cilla wasn't worried at all. She giggled, happily clapping her hands. "Slow down, dogs." Dolfe commanded firmly. "I don't think anybody called all five of you."

The canine squad screeched to a halt and

plopped to their bottoms to stare up at Dolfe, clearly assuming since they were irresistible and Dolfe was a human and therefore a slave to their every whim, food would be coming their way shortly.

They were about to be disappointed.

Totally unconcerned with his intimidating presence, Ivy slipped through Dolfe's legs with a jaunty step that told him the little dog had way too much confidence and leapt into the chair. She landed on Cilla and Blaise, spurring much happy giggling.

"It looks like the dogs have already bonded," Brita said from behind Dolfe.

He turned to smile at her. "I think we have a new rat pack in the works."

Brita scratched Darth Dane's big, soft ears and gave him a kiss in the wide space between his eyes. The back door of the house slammed shut and she lost the food-motivated baby as he turned to bound toward Clovis and Emma. The big ex-Marine was carrying a tray mounded with steaks and Emma had a large bowl of something green and leafy.

At the sound of Darth's giant-sized *woof*, the other dogs took off like a shot after him. Ivy gave Cilla a final kiss on the nose and jumped down to join her new pack.

Brita grinned after them, laughing unhelpfully as Clovis made a panicked sound and lifted the tray high over his head and then jumped in front of a laughing Emma. "I never get enough of this."

"There's definitely something heart healthy about watching the dogs play," Blaise agreed with a soft smile.

Percy Honeybun walked up to them with three icy beers, handing one to Brita and one to Dini. "I have to admit, I worried about having five dogs..." He pulled Brita under one arm and kissed her on the cheek. "But I'm loving it."

Dolfe shook his head. "I can't imagine five of them. Miss Ivy keeps us on our toes."

Blaise stood up, settling Cilla onto the ground so she could run after the dogs. "She is a handful, but on the plus side, she's forcing me to get some exercise."

"We walk her twice a day," Dolfe agreed. "She's already won the hearts of almost all our neighbors."

"Almost?" Dini asked, cocking her head and grinning.

Blaise rolled her eyes. "There always has to be one crotchety, 'get off my lawn' guy on the street."

Brita nodded. "Word."

"So, Brita," Dolfe said, "what's going on with the White case?"

"Yeah, I promised I'd give you the wrap-up didn't I?"

Blaise nodded, her brown gaze filled with interest. "Hopefully you had enough to charge those horrible women with murder?"

"And abduction," Brita said.

"Any surprises?" Dolfe asked.

"Not really. As you suspected, the whole thing started when Georgina Sands was overlooked by her husband to run *Artisan Beers*. She didn't take kindly to that at all, but realized since the business was technically her husband's baby, she couldn't force her way into the position. Instead, she started to hatch a plot to discredit Kopper."

Blaise frowned. "But even if she got rid of Kopper, her husband could have just hired somebody else."

"True." Brita nodded. "But she figured she'd step into the role as acting manager and once she'd proved herself her husband wouldn't want her to step down."

"Delusional much?" Dolfe murmured.

"Yeah, she was that and so much more," Brita sighed. "Crazy land. She lost her job with the FBI because she had serious anger issues and very little respect for boundaries."

"I'm surprised she didn't just kill Kopper," Blaise mused. "She didn't seem to have any problem killing just about everybody else who crossed her path."

"I'm guessing the only thing holding her back was the fear that her husband would figure out she'd killed Kopper for his job."

"And D?" Blaise asked. "Who tried to kill her both times?"

Brita frowned. "D? Oh, you mean Deirdre? It was

Georgina Sands. Once we knew it was her we were able to match ballistics to the sidearm she had when she was with the Feds. She tried to kill Deirdre in her car and, when that didn't work, she went to the hospital, dressed in her 'guy' outfit and tried to smother her."

Dolfe chuckled. "Don't tell me Georgina Sands drives a souped-up muscle car?"

"No," Brita shook her head. "The car she ran Deirdre Masterson off the road with belonged to Sparks."

They fell silent for a beat, probably all thinking the same thing. It was a miracle Deirdre Masterson had fought off two deadly attempts on her life.

"Okay, so who abducted Suz?" Dolfe asked.

"Ginny told me she did it but I have trouble picturing her dragging Suz out of the bar. They were about the same size," Blaise said on a frown.

"Right," Dolfe said. "And Sparks's van was seen leaving that morning."

Brita nodded. "Sparks was waiting up the street for Ginny and, when Ginny ran into trouble with Suz she called him to come help. Sparks did put Suz into that van and take her into the country, but Ginny was the one who attacked her inside the bar. She'd gone there to get rid of evidence that would point to her poisoning Roger White. Unfortunately, Suz walked in on her and Ginny had to hide. She ducked into the storage room, hoping Suz would leave without finding her. Sadly, it didn't quite work out that way."

"Why did Ginny even get involved?" Dolfe asked. "It makes no sense."

"She wanted Roger's job and thought she was just as qualified as he was," Blaise told him.

"Not really." Brita disagreed. "She had a couple of years of biochemistry but she didn't have a knack for it. Her C minus grades didn't exactly inspire Tabitha Clear to hire her as a lab tech."

"How did the two women get together?" Percy asked.

Brita glanced up at him. "Apparently the plot was hatched at the annual Micro-Brewer's Conference. They planned to force Kopper out at *Artisan* and, once Georgina got control of the brewery, she was going to hire Ginny to work in their Brew Lab."

Blaise shook her head. "I can't believe those two killed three people and almost killed Suz and me just to get better jobs."

"Like I said...Crazy land," Brita agreed.

"How did Sparks get pulled into the plot?" Dolfe asked.

"Well, as you guessed, he was her nephew but they were never close. She knew he wasn't happy about the newly popular microbrew scene at his favorite bar and she used that to entice him into helping her."

"What was in it for him?" Blaise asked.

"Money. Georgina promised him a big payout if he helped her clean up the mess Roger White caused by threatening to go to the FDA with the tainted beer sample."

"Yeah, what was up with that?" Blaise asked. "Was he actually blackmailing Kopper? Why did he keep that report?"

"According to Ginny, Roger went to Tabatha and told her he wanted to send the result to the FDA. Tabatha apparently told him to destroy the sample and the report and stay out of it. She promised him she'd speak to Artie Sands."

"And Roger kept a copy as a CYA," Dolfe speculated.

"Exactly. He had nothing to do with the blackmail. His only thing was that he hated Kopper with a passion. It was the reason he scored Artisan's samples so rigidly. Tabatha's relationship with Sands didn't help either. Apparently she was always protecting him and that rubbed Roger the wrong way."

Blaise nodded. "It doesn't speak well for the company's integrity and, since he was a shareholder in *Clear Brew*, he stood to lose more than his job."

"But I don't understand," Dini piped in. "If these women were trying to get rid of Kopper, wouldn't it make sense to just let Roger White turn him into the FDA?"

"No," Brita said. "Because it wouldn't just be

Roger who went down if he did that. *Artisan Beers* would be toast. They wanted to scare Kopper off or get him arrested for murder but they didn't want him to take the company down with him."

"They surely did everything in their power to point the finger of blame toward him," Dolfe said, shaking his head. "And he helped by acting guilty."

Blaise shook her head. "What a mess. I'm just glad it's over."

"Enough business talk," Clovis said, walking up and handing Dolfe a container of seasoning and a pair of tongs. "You're up on the barbeque."

"What are you gonna do while I'm slaving over a hot fire?"

Clovis grinned. "I'm going to go throw the football with my brothers."

They all turned to the area across the acre-sized yard where the Honeybun boys and their honeys had set up a flag football field. From what Dolfe could see the flags were pretty much useless, since the men seemed to prefer slamming into and taking each other down instead.

"I guess I know why I was invited to the party," Dolfe groused good-naturedly.

Clovis clapped him on the back. "Stop whining soldier. That wasn't the only reason." He grabbed Blaise and tugged her into a hug as she laughed. "We needed a quarterback and your future wife was my first pick."

Clovis grabbed a shrieking Dini too and pulled her under his other arm. "Come on Princess Chandini. I believe you were instructed to report for assignment an hour ago."

Feeling as if he'd been taken, Dolfe watched them head across the yard.

"Blaise *is* a really good quarterback, Brita said, laughing.

"How about if I grab you another beer?" Percy asked, his blue eyes sparkling with humor.

Dolfe handed him his empty. "Thanks, cuz. I'm glad somebody knows how to take care of the cook."

"I'll take another one too," Brita called out as Percy headed toward the cooler on the patio. She followed Dolfe to the grill and sat down in a chair a few feet away. "So tell me about the exotic animal ring case. Have you made any progress?"

Dolfe checked a couple of the steaks, turned the heat down a little, and dusted the sizzling meat with the seasoning as he started filling Brita in on his newest and most frustrating case. She interjected a few times, giving him ideas on how to direct the investigation, and Dolfe soon found himself lost in the challenge of the hunt.

The sun shone down, hot and golden, the trees rustled under a perfect breeze and the scent of newly mown grass competed with the delicious scent of grilling meat to create his perfect moment.

Behind him Miss Ivy yipped, setting off a multidog zoomie fest with a wildly giggling Cilla bringing up the rear and he laughed, feeling as if, in that precise moment, his world was just about as idyllic as it could possibly be.

Especially when he caught his future wife's happy gaze across the yard. And he realized he might just be the luckiest man alive.

Thanks so much for reading Blaise and Dolfe's story! I hope you enjoyed **Murderous Craft** and if you can post a quick review of the book I'd greatly appreciate it.

If you'd like to read more Blaise and Dolfe mysteries, Book 3: **Fatal Assignment** is available for purchase now!

A temporary office assignment turns deadly. And Blaise quickly finds herself in a killer's crosshairs.

Backstabbing, infidelity, greed and power. There's nothing more dangerous than office intrigue. Blaise continues her search for the perfect career by taking a temporary assignment in an architectural firm. Though she quickly learns that wrangling a proposal team to get to end of project is nearly impossible, keeping everyone alive might just be the hardest thing she'll ever do.

With the help of her sexy fiancé, Dolfe Honeybun, Blaise is determined to get to the bottom of the body in the elevator. Problem is, with a cast of suspects longer than her *To Do* list, Blaise is up to her perfectly plucked eyebrows in possible killers. And she might not know who the killer is, but he knows everything there is to know about Blaise

Get Fatal Assignment!

FATAL ASSIGNMENT

Blaise Runa checked her make-up in the mirror for the last time and climbed out of her car. Her phone rang as she started across the nearly empty parking lot to the ugly brick and metal building squatting alongside the street. The sun was still a vague promise on the horizon and Blaise felt the usual mix of excitement and dread as she approached the smudged glass doors leading to the lobby of the *Beck and Poole Architectural Firm*.

She tugged her phone from her purse and looked down, smiling at the photo of her newest love, Miss Ivy, the big eared, sweet tempered mutt she and Dolfe recently adopted. Blaise punched the *Answer* button. "Hey, Handsome."

"Morning, future wife. I couldn't believe you were already gone when I woke up. Third time this week."

Blaise pulled a lanyard free of her sweater and lifted the key card on the end, swiping it across the reader to unlock the door. "I have two days to get this proposal together and I'm still missing several pieces. I'm going to have to hit the database hard and try to pull together something for the team to edit."

Heavy breathing came through the phone and Blaise blinked in surprise. "Are you giving me stalker breath?"

Dolfe's husky chuckle replaced the breathing, followed by a wet slurp and a tiny yip. "Oh, is that Ivy?"

Another yip. "High, baby! Mama's got to work today. You be good for Daddy, okay?"

She could almost hear Dolfe rolling his eyes. "You know she's a dog, right?"

"I'm aware. But she's my little fur baby too."

"If she's *your* baby then that makes her *my* baby and I don't want to claim a baby this ugly."

Blaise hit the stairs, eschewing the elevator in an attempt to skim the few extra pounds she'd piled on since taking the temporary project management position a few weeks earlier. The building had a killer cafeteria, with the world's best pastries.

It was going to be the death of her.

"I hope you covered her ears before you called her ugly. She's very sensitive."

He snorted. "Sensitive? This little monster thinks

she rules the world. She doesn't have a sensitive bone in her puny little body."

Blaise grinned. He wasn't wrong. Ivy might only weigh ten pounds, but she thought she was a lion. "Give her a kiss for me, will you? I'll see you tonight?"

"That'll be a hard *No* on the kiss and a gooey *Yes* on the seeing me later part."

"Love ya, babe."

"I love you too, honey. But I have one more thing to say..."

"What's that?" Blaise tugged the door open to the office on the third floor where she had a desk and flipped on the light.

"If we're this monster's parents, you're taking the blame for these ears."

She was still laughing moments later when she reached her desk. Blaise dropped her purse into an oversized drawer and draped her sweater over the back of her chair. The temperature of the room was kept in the mid-seventies at all times and she was already hot. She stood at the window that ran the entire length of the building on the south-facing side, overlooking the parking lot.

Her cute little sports car, a recent gift from Dolfe, sat beneath the brightest light on the edge of the lot. She'd taken to parking out there to keep dings to a minimum. The well-lighted area also ensured the sexy little car would be safe from tampering after business hours.

Blaise forced herself away from the window, determined to make progress on her missing proposal sections by the time the team showed up for work at eight am. She headed for the break room and started a pot of coffee.

While she waited for the coffee to brew, Blaise scanned the cupboards for something to eat. She hadn't taken time for breakfast before she left. There were some small boxes of sugary cereal but no milk, and some cartons of fat-free yogurt in the fridge. Blaise shrugged. She could make do with that.

As the coffee pot spurted its last, Blaise ripped the top off the cereal box and stretched it into a more circular shape. Then she opened the yogurt and dumped it into the foil-lined box. She found a plastic spoon and grabbed a paper towel before pouring herself a cup of coffee and heading back to her desk with her makeshift breakfast.

While her computer warmed up, she ate thoughtfully, perusing her notes for the content the team needed to complete the proposal that was due the following day at five pm.

Somewhere downstairs a door slammed closed and Blaise jumped.

The cafeteria crew must have arrived. She briefly considered heading down for a cheese Danish but then mentally slapped herself. At the rate she was going, she wasn't going to fit into the wedding dress she hadn't picked out yet.

Instead, Blaise scooted her chair closer to her desk and set to work on the database.

This data won't work, it's too outdated."

Blaise glanced down the conference table to focus what she hoped was a professional look on the speaker. Walton Hunt was an arrogant, thirty-something Services tech who spent more time every day trying to get out of actually doing any work than he did performing his job.

She bit back an angry response and gave him a tight smile. "That's because it's boilerplate content, Walton. I just wanted to give you something to rewrite for your assigned section."

He shook his head, flinging the binder she'd put together for him away. It hit the table with a jarring thud and everyone at the table flinched. "I can't work with this. You're going to have to come up with a more targeted response."

Blaise saw red. She'd been fighting with several departments since the beginning to get them to write their sections of the proposal. She'd managed to wrangle a few of them into giving her what she needed, but Hunt had refused. Which was why she'd succumbed to using the daily team meeting to put pressure on him. "I'm not an architect, Walton. I don't have the training or experience to write a more targeted response. That's why you're here."

His handsome face turned red and he leaned forward, clearly believing he could scare her with his bully tactics.

Blaise leaned forward too, her gaze locked unwaveringly on his. *Bring it, jerk!* she thought.

"Walton, let's examine this at a thirty-thousand-foot level." Vanessa Puget reached a well-manicured hand toward the binder Walton Hunt had thrown and pulled it closer, opening it to the spot Blaise had carefully marked for him. As the Client Executive for the customer account to whom they were presenting the proposal, Vanessa was the team lead. From what Blaise had heard, she was very good at her job and mostly that was because she was good with people.

But as Walton's hostile gaze narrowed on Blaise, his square jaw taut with rage, Blaise figured Vanessa might have met her match. "I'm not taking orders from this...this...temp on how to do my job," he growled.

Vanessa threw Blaise an apologetic look. "Blaise is just trying to do what we hired her for. It's her job to manage the multitude of pieces required for this proposal into a single, effective and persuasive document."

"We don't need a PM for this job," a man

named Alex Montrose whined. Alex studiously avoided Blaise's gaze as he flipped the corners of the pages in his binder. "We need someone who understands this client's specific needs and hot buttons."

Vanessa's smile appeared strained. "That would be us, Alex. We all have a piece of the puzzle that needs to be included. I'm client facing, trying to pin them down on what we can give them that will win us this deal. Walton needs to give us the technical piece. You, Alex, owe Blaise the Statement of Work response. And Alice needs to complete the Human Resources section." Her head suddenly came up and she looked around the table. "Anybody know where Doug is?"

Doug Watts was the pricer for the proposal. He'd been a no-show for most of the meetings and had refused to respond to Blaise's attempts to reach out via email or phone. Blaise shook her head. "He never responded to the meeting invite."

Vanessa scrubbed a hand over her face, sighing. "Okay, I'll track him down." She scoured the table with a look. "Each of you has a vital piece of this thing. We need to lock it down no later than tomorrow morning's meeting because Blaise needs to print everything up and get a dozen copies into binders in time for me to deliver it to the client by five pm. Understand?"

Everyone but Walton nodded. He was glowering

at the binder on the table, his jaw jutting belligerently.

Vanessa scanned Blaise a look as everyone stood up to leave. "Blaise, can you hang back for a few minutes? I want to go over final production with you."

"Sure."

The other woman waited until the team left the room and then went to close the door behind them. She stood in front of the door for a moment, her expression worried. "I'm terrified we're not going to be able to wrangle these guys into action in time."

Blaise shared the same fear. "What can I do to help?"

"Can you write the entire proposal and price it for me?" Vanessa's smile was tight, without humor. "I've got calls in to Walton's and Doug's managers. Hopefully they'll be able to apply the right kind of pressure. But there's just no time."

"I can try to find more targeted content in the database. Just in case."

Vanessa thought about Blaise's suggestion and sighed. "Okay. If we need to we'll go with less focused content and I'll just have to work harder in the negotiation stage." She gave Blaise a smile. "Thanks. You've been a godsend."

Blaise nodded. She genuinely liked the other woman. "I'm happy to help."

"The way Walton and some of the others have

treated you, I'm surprised you haven't gone running for the hills by now."

"Nah. I don't like bullies. The more they try to get rid of me the more I dig in."

Vanessa laughed. "I like your style."

Blaise gave the other woman a wide smile. "Besides, there's the cafeteria..."

Vanessa snorted out a laugh. "I swear, I've gained ten pounds since I came to work here."

"You must have been too skinny then because you're just about perfect now."

Flushing with pleasure, Vanessa sat down and pulled a pad of paper closer. "I'll give you some keywords for the content we need. They'll help you get a closer match to the solution we're proposing to *Aldred Industries*. Also, look at the proposal I did in February, *Massey and Klinder Law Offices*. That one was very similar."

Blaise jotted down the information, her mind already going over the boilerplate she'd seen in the database to consider possibilities. When Vanessa left for a client meeting Blaise headed back to her desk.

Her stomach began rumbling a few hours later. Blaise grabbed her purse from the bottom drawer and started for the door. The big room filled with desks and cubicles was nearly empty. Clearly, she was one of the last to leave for lunch.

Alice Moss from HR was heading out of her office when Blaise pulled the door open. She held it for the other woman and received a friendly smile for her trouble. "Thanks, honey. Are you heading downstairs?"

"I am. I think they have cream of chicken soup today."

Alice nodded. "I had some earlier. It was delicious."

"I'm thinking there might be a giant rice krispies treat in my future too."

Laughing, Alice patted her hip. "I wish I could indulge. I'll see you later." The other woman headed for the stairs. Blaise had seen her using them more often lately and figured she was probably on an exercise spree.

"See ya later." Blaise stopped in front of the elevator. "Hey?"

Alice stopped with her hand on the stairwell door, a smile on her plain face. "Yes?"

"You'll have those responses to me by five tonight?"

Alice lifted the slender binder she held in her left hand. "I will. You have my word."

"Great." Blaise gave the woman a genuine smile as the doors slid open with a ding. "Thanks so much, Alice."

"My pleasure, sweetie. You know..."

Blaise hesitated, her hand on the doors to hold them open.

"You're doing a good job. Don't let those jerks tell you otherwise."

A bloom of pure pleasure swept Blaise. She nodded and stepped onto the elevator, feeling the smile widening on her face as it descended toward the lobby.

Check out all the Gainfully Employed Mysteries: https://www.samcheever.com/series.html#gainfullye mployed

ALSO BY SAM CHEEVER

If you enjoyed **Murderous Craft**, you might also enjoy these other fun mystery series by Sam. To find out more, visit the **BOOKS** page at www.samcheever.com:

Gainfully Employed Mysteries

Honeybun Heat Series

Silver Hills Cozy Mysteries

Country Cousin Mysteries

Yesterday's Paranormal Mysteries

Reluctant Familiar Paranormal Mysteries

ABOUT THE AUTHOR

USA Today and Wall Street Journal Bestselling Author Sam Cheever writes mystery and suspense, creating stories that draw you in and keep you eagerly turning pages. Known for writing great characters, snappy dialogue, and unique and exhilarating stories, Sam is the award-winning author of 80+ books.

To learn more about Sam and her work, visit her at one of her online hotspots:
www.samcheever.com
samcheever@samcheever.com